ABOUT FACE

About Face

SHORT FICTION

BY

CECILE ROSSANT

RED HEN PRESS 🐓 LOS ANGELES

for Jerry,

Like the chance that you hooked this book —

Hook —

See you soon —

Enjoy the Book

Cecil

Nov. 4 '07

BERLIN

Cover photograph *Interior No. 1*
by Nanae Suzuki

Book design by James M.J. Harmon
Cover Design by Mark E. Cull

ISBN 1-888996-20-X

Library of Congress Catalog Card Number 2004095867

Published by Red Hen Press

The City of Los Angeles Cultural Affairs Department,
California Arts Council and
the Los Angeles County Arts Commission
partially support Red Hen Press.

First Edition

Acknowledgments

I owe my deepest thanks to Edith Ferber whose grace and
generosity provided the ground for the realization of this book.

I am very grateful to—
Kate Gale and Mark E. Cull for their invitation to make this book
and their patient commitment to its realization, Marianne Rossant:
her careful reading and insightful editorial comments were true
gifts, Colette and James Rossant, two steady readers, whose
thoughtful suggestions and unwavering encouragement have helped
in a myriad of ways, and to Rajesh Mehta, for opening my ears, and
Celine, Caio and Christian for their refreshing love.

Contents

Mandarin   1

About Face   2

Infatuation   7

Plans and Elevations   10

The Tuna Club   12

An Overheard   17

Real Estate   18

Today's Performance   20

On My Way Home   21

The Appointment   28

Leila's Friends   30

Once and Again   35

The Knoll   36

Officer P   37

Untitled   40

The Woman   41

She Twists to Position Her Face   42

Escape   55

I Was Sitting Alone   56

Monopoly   57

Child   61

Suburban Rodeo   62

Baby Beckett   66

Horizontal Drainage   67

An Open Mouth   74

Earthworms   75

It Comes with the Job   76

Viewfinder   77

Sequence   80

Heavenly Bodies   81

The Face   83

The Daughter Wakes Up From the
    Dream of Emerging from Her
    Father's Head   84

The Head   85

The Belly of a Bird   86

She Hisses 'til He Kisses Her 'air   109

The Identity Card   112

through my quick-rising voice to your quick-hearing ear, Ghen!

Mandarin

The orange's eye watches my heartless moment of
activity.
Heartless activity condenses into pendulous
droplets underscoring an indicative but imprecise
rhythm.
The droplets collect in the day's plateau and
assume the shape of an orange complete with peel
and sections as example.

About Face

I loved a man. We made love on the floor and fell asleep. When I woke, he was nearly dead. In a frenzy, unfamiliar with the faces of death, I tried to nurse him back, but it was too late. He met the day with a seizure; he rattled and then froze.

An ambulance arrived; I traveled with his body, still believing there was something that could bring him back alive.

Later on, when I was telling the whole story to the police, I noticed the smell.

The smell of our lovemaking had dripped out of me and had dried as a perfumed patch on his sweatpants. I had had no time to wash or to wear my own clothes.

An ethereal substance wafted up to my face each time my legs fanned open. Something rose, and caused me to falter. But most of all I so forcefully remembered the vessel, the descending path to the vessel: the vase with open mouth where his vitality still had its temporary lodging and dimensionality, and from which it was now flowing out and evaporating.

Many years later, impressionistically rendered again, I was astounded that I had been that bearer, that I was fitted with another's teeming life . . . momentarily, but also undeniably formed and borne.

A corridor. At a closed door the walking stops and turns. Behind the door is a linoleum lined room with several plastic chairs, a thin table and an opening to the adjoining room. The two uniformed men following me wheeled in his body.

Before the police arrived, they assembled the box made of a light, evenly grained wood, there, in the room, from a prefabricated kit. The white kimono was slipped out of its clear plastic wrapping and they dressed him with difficulty.

Ahead is a large window framed by an edge of the room, then the ceiling, and the floor.

The readied box was set atop the table and rolled up to his body. The two men and his brother signaled their mutual preparedness and lifted and lowered his body into the box. I wailed. I protested. I refused to accept his being boxed. There was no choice and my protest had no effect on the sequence of events.

The adjoining room was fitted with a raised floor and a low centered table. After I had quieted down, we all entered the room and sat on the floor, leaving our shoes one step below. The police, his brother, uncle, aunt and I sat around the low table like family. They had questions, and their questions soon became my questions.

I told them that while at work in the office yesterday, relocating books, he fell from a ladder when a bookshelf collapsed. He told me that last night.

One of the policemen directed another to call the office. I gave them the telephone number. The phone was handed to me and I spoke to the secretary. She said she knew nothing of his fall. I told her to find out who had been there with him. I told her to ask everyone. I spoke emphatically. For a moment I was ready to accuse someone. I was even tapping through the phone.

The night before, we stood beside the sink while he told me the story. I ran my fingers through his hair and felt the small swelling. But I don't really remember doing this. I have no recollection of the bump. I led him away from the kitchen sink to the apartment's only room, through the doorless threshold, as if leading him away from his story, the only manifested alert, away from the inertia of my concern that would beg me to take an action to stop the onset of dread.

And I think so often about how little we know about the body on the inside: when damaged and when not, when dying and when not . . .

I spoke to them until I stopped. All of this while his body lay still and silent in the adjacent room.

To me, a coffin is only a box: to put away something, to keep the body out of sight, so the thing can't work on you anymore. The box is a practical way to conceal a transition, one that we have judged too hard to handle. So we simply stop "handling" the body, which only hours before had some control over how it wished to be touched.

In this sense, a dead body is helpless; this is exactly why it needs to be handled with extreme care and attentiveness. But our society has given up on this responsibility; consequently, a recently dead body is put in a box so it can be stored temporarily, positioned and repositioned with practical ease. When I saw the two uniformed men and his brother move towards him with intent to lift him into the box, I had to be restrained.

Hiss! Nested boxes of compressed dust coated with layers of paint are connected by openings through which the smaller, flatter boxes may be passed from one functional chamber to another. Toward the inner core is the one made of thin interlocking wood planks banged together; a firm fingernail can leave shallow traces on either type of surface.

I slide open the door of my room. His parents told me this would be my room as long as I was in their house. Its door slides open onto the living room where his coffin lies. The wood box is beside the large window and raised above the floor.

At night his mother and father, his two brothers, and his grandparents sleep in the house's other rooms. I said goodnight several times and closed the door behind me.

I peel back the covers. The door slides open. Shoeless, I flow into the living room. I'm stopped by the wall. I open the small window on the coffin's lid. Its entire cover can also be turned back on its hinge. I spoke with him for several hours and didn't return to my room except to retrieve my cover. This living room had a sofa positioned at right angles to the box. Eventually I closed my eyes. I left the living room light on the entire night. I leaned in, my face close to his—exactly how or if I touched him is difficult to remember.

Does the art of touching have its limits? I'm still drawn to inscribe my caress on his many faces. Now he is all ears.

While burning we/the party of people/we, the gathered/were upstairs. There was food and discussion. It was a lively scene with talking, with references/with reference to him and ourselves. It was a modern building: mainstays of concrete and sheets of glass. He was wheeled in, still in a box. Chromed steel elevator doors opened. He was pushed in and the doors closed behind him.

Bones. I crushed his bones. We did it. But I remember what I did. His family had invited me to join in the ritual. I participated with an enthusiasm that to the others must have appeared uncanny—extreme. I was unreserved. Grandfather absent, we struck the bones with the wooden mallet until we had a small white pile of chips and flakes between us. A bit more and the chips became dust and fine gravel. The crushed bone was returned to the urn. I helped, using my hands to gather whatever I could. Across from the counter where we worked was a fountain with running water to rinse the hands. His mother led me there: she turned me and pushed me gently toward the tap. But I turned back again as if it wasn't enough; I wasn't yet ready to wash. I rubbed my face with dusty hands, and as I have said, I would have licked my fingers. I would have consumed him by the spoonful: edible or inedible I would have swallowed him—so ravenous was I for that intimacy. And by the way, the room in which we stood, like six actors on a stage, was small and well lit. It opened directly onto the lobby of the crematorium where the rest of the party was watching and waiting. But I couldn't care less about any of them.

The box burst; it's busted. The skin burnt to an inescapably fragile crisp. It traveled up with the current and floated down, twirling and dusting the ground.

It should be sung to the sound of fire—

(The ritual that failed to happen: one that has been compromised and ignored by an entire society, collectively, until the ritual is effectively outlawed.)

The site: the top of a gently sloping swell in the ground—in a plain, preferably at a distance from tree groupings. Sufficient wood is stacked for the fire to burn seven hours or more. Above the stacked logs is a sisal mat.

The actual source of heat is unimportant, but the fire is not.

His body was swaddled in a simple cloth: his legs bound together, while his arms, wrapped individually, were placed on top of his body, uncrossed, with his hands resting on his hips or slightly higher up, allowing bent elbows. A narrow strip of cloth spanning crosswise held his hands in place. The cloth covering his face and ears is of a lighter weave, resembling gauze. It burns away so rapidly without leaving a cast of itself.

He was anointed with oils. Guided by an experienced healer, she massaged the oils into his body and hair-covered head according to the most effective pattern. They carried him to the burning site, laid him on the mat and tied him down to the pyre.

The one who tended to him, from this point on, never left his body. Another one lit the fire. When she needed drink, her mouth dry from speaking and her throat roughened by the smoke, water was poured from above in a stream, into her mouth, and kept clear from the flames.

Whether the period of burning was scripted or unscripted was according to the choice of the attendant.

Infatuation

Ma is her name. She is at the end—standing at the end of the hall or seated beside his bed watching the TV screen until the last of the credits scroll by—and the beginning.

Because Ma is always waiting for the slightest acknowledgement of her presence, she hears the beginning of every one of his utterances with the utmost clarity. "Ma! When you go to Ed's, buy me a box of cigarettes." She precedes Lem. For Ma, being there for his beginning was akin to witnessing a miracle.

I caused a dilemma when I dragged Di to Lem who was lying near enough but who was just too lethargic etceteras, to get up to meet her on his own accord. He is the type to stay in bed, even starve in bed, so long as he has enough cigarettes to fend off hunger and enough stamina to bring on and hold an erection if a beautiful woman happens to stroll by. I came too late.

If ever he is forced to earn some money to pay for his fully blossomed smoking habit he refuses to handle any material except metals. He believes anything else, and perhaps rightly, will speed up his physical decay, or even more repugnant, coat him in the unbearable film of its own deterioration.

Lem once explained that metallic by-products inlay the skin in an oily metallic dust that he thinks acts as a preservative. He works for weeks at a time at a die manufacturing plant nearby. On break, he often rubs the machine oil into his hands, face and forearms, and down the front and sides of his jeans. I have loved Lem, presumably for his supreme detachment, which I have been perpetually unable to achieve. He needs few categories for things and even fewer for states of being.

I have wondered at times that he probably doesn't even recognize that chickens with their heads axed off are hopping around the planet . . . somewhere.

Today Lem showered. To do so he stands in the dark hallway of his apartment. The shower is a length of rubber surgical hose, hardened and darkened with age. He attaches the hose to a joint in the water pipe and loosens the outer ring. Water leaks through the joint. He lifts away the floorboards beneath his shower. Standing on two exposed joists, he directs the water dripping off his body to the gap between. The apartment beneath his is abandoned. A couple of months ago, Lem positioned a metal basin below the hole to catch the falling water. Lem smokes as he showers. "I would fucking freeze otherwise," he says. The ashes also fall through the hole in the floor.

Di is not worth talking about. She serves something as crass as other people's interest in her body. I am not unkind to her. If Lem asks me to bring her to his place, I never refuse. But we don't have much to say. We really have nothing in common. For example, I can't share in her understanding of Lem—not at all.

Di is beautiful. She has a kind of beauty that hooks into you. I stare at her when we ride the train together. I am not even sure what I am thinking about. She sits across from me cross-legged and bobs her floating leg up and down like a dog. That disturbs everyone on the train. I can see that some of them would give a lot just to touch her with the tip of a finger. They can't grasp how little she has to offer. For Di, intensity always wins over complexity. I can't accept that kind of selfishness.

She and Lem don't talk at all. In exclusive concentration they move towards each other with controlled and efficient movement, like dancers . . .

It's not that I hang around to watch. It's something I understand afterwards, when Di has already left. It is the way Lem pins himself to the bed after she leaves, as though he wants to remember how each part of him was involved in the performance that they just completed. Lying there, Lem draws a mental picture of himself. He likes what he sees.

Thinking about their relation sends shivers down my back. I have to walk somewhere, fast, to a public place. Five blocks away is a diner. I order coffee and read the long menu and the paper if it's available. When the place gets crowded I ask for a danish, a small salad or a large tomato juice. I never want to eat something that might put me to sleep. In a little while, I am seeing other couplings. Once it was the cook's hands cracking eggs, tossing fries, managing a pen and his burgers. Last time, Sunday afternoon, I couldn't stop looking at the plastic flowers in the window. How the leaves bounced every time someone left or entered the place.

Today's waitress refills my cup. I stay seated for a sip or two.

Lem is not at home. I have his keys that I use only after ringing his bell at least 10 times. Six months ago I accidentally walked in on Di and Lem. They didn't notice me. Both lay on the bed in Christ on the Cross positions—Lem flat on top of Di. It was so quiet I could hear their even, heavy breathing. They were barely moving. Unfortunately, I picked up on the caterpillar-segment-like movement of Lem's sweet behind and knew that they were joined. I tiptoed down the hall; the floorboards creaked. I didn't dare look around; one view of them together was good enough for a lifetime.

Luckily, today Lem left the window open. A fresh wind blew across the room. This morning I bought artificial flowers and throw them on his bed just to check their effect.

I'm staring at the flowers when Lem walks in. He lies right on top and closes his eyes. His long hair falls across the pink and yellow petals. His smile rises on a face lit by a warm orange glow. Later, the face is ashen blue. I want to pull him out of bed, but I just sit there until the sun goes down. The room is in almost total darkness when Lem finally sits up, lights a cigarette and says hello.

Plans and Elevations

Awoken by an already awoken body, one already sweaty from some unknown exertion in a shared bed beside a nondescript huddle of quilt and head, I drew my finger across the pooled moisture between my breasts and tuned into his snoring.

Can you imagine waking and immediately cursing the thoughts and contortions of emotion that drove you to lie in a shared bed? This is exactly what I did. Within this onslaught of regret the image of the square bed notched with two dark marks connoting our supposedly resting bodies rose with a swoosh and turned on me, now as a convenient pictogram. I quickly understood this symbolic figure could join many formulations in the world at large.

I discovered a narrow brick wall—too wide for me to wrap my arms around, standing upright beside me in bed. I slipped around it in order to leave the room. You could say that it reached the ceiling, that it was fixed in place, but it's not that important if it does or can, because it appears rigid and fixed in place.

At times I hallucinate that the wall has nearly the same dimensions as I do. It does have handholds. This illusion leads to further delusions, because I've assumed that it would leave the building and tunnel headlong down the street into the abundance of addresses.

But it fixes itself to other rooms—its means of attachment so subtle: perhaps nothing more than just being there—even when leaning out of windows.

It's rather tall, the wall, at least when on the bed—that in this position it reaches the ceiling.

Suffice it to say, I take advantage of its stability to slip around between it and the wall, into the abundance of addresses.

If a structure is damaged in countless places and in fact deteriorated to such a degree that it seems pointless to even plan its renovation, sooner or later the pavement will be torn out and carted away. After the occupants pack up and relocate—the wrecking ball will swing against its walls changing the building into rubble piles, which are also carted away.

The Tuna Club

Kang was one of those flowers with thin susceptible petals. Trembling white, yellow to snowy white petals, easily plucked from a center button, leave behind a whorl of empty horns around a slowly drying mound. Such a male has the taste of dust: a perfumed powdery pollen on his tongue, and embedded nodules in the wet fertile ground of his inner cheeks.

For the past two weeks, in order to finish the midyear progress report, no one in Kang's department left the building until midnight. A box of printed brochures was delivered late Friday afternoon and every married man on the floor called his wife.

As the group was exceptionally large that evening, the accounting department made a preparatory visit to their regular drinking hole to relax and to get on familiar terms with one another. The danger existed that the awkward stiffness of the junior staff would spoil a good time at the outrageously expensive and exclusive club.

It took less than half an hour before most of their faces were deeply flushed, with lips oiled and moistened by the string of small dishes of food and the beer and whisky brought to the table. Kang heard several speeches and an innumerable number of toasts. By the time it was dangerously close to the time that it would no longer be possible to attend the evening's main attraction, the project manager motioned the waiter. Several of the senior staff loosened their ties and wiped the sweat from their brows.

The accounting department stumbled out onto the street. Mid-July and the sticky air did little to sharpen each man's profile. At least one in the group knew the way. He led the men down a side street to the newly built Nikki-to building. The street's reflection fell off the building's black glass surface as they slipped through sliding doors into the lobby, which was little more than a narrow, mirrored corridor with a pair of elevator doors cut into the center of one wall. The ten penguins split into two teams that stood single file on either side of the elevators. Each kept still in an effort to avoid gesturing to his own reflection. The elevators arrived simultaneously

12

and the two groups entered the cabins repeating the chorus, "Hey, sixth floor, sixth floor, sixth floor, O.K.—"

Pats on the back circulated as they were reunited.

A petite, evenly tanned hostess in stretchy pink and white, detailed with miniature pearls, greets the men. Her well-manicured fingers bring the penguins through the tiled door and seat them in the dark and shiny upholstered den. A whisky bottle pulled off the wall initiates another round of drinks while the hostess sprinkles the bar with indelicate flattery and salty snacks.

After a short while, she tells one of the older boys to knock on the little door there. Her thin lips hover between a patronizing provocation and a barely concealed disgust. He grins to the rest as he does her bid. A plump girl-girl masquerading as a bunny answers the call. Emerging out from under the door's low cut frame, she straightens up, kisses the old boy's sweaty cheek and turns a loose pirouette. Apart from her pink and white ears, two furry white tufts decorate her breasts, a string panty of white fur hoists up and separates her cheeks and two clumps attached to her red-heeled feet complete her costume perfectly. As she bears down into a bow, demonstrating the suspended form of her fur-tipped breasts, the penguins hoot and rock in their seats from buttock to buttock. *Well, go on in boys*—says the hostess, gesturing to the small door. The girl-girl's bowing becomes a bubbly bobbing as the penguins rise and file by, stooping down to pass through the door. Each finds a place to settle down in the black mirrored booth where another girl-girl is waiting.

There is a round of introductions. Glasses are filled and the pretty bunnies take turns feeding the penguins peanuts. The girl-girls kneel on molded pillows raised above the seated men. Then the real fun begins. Aoki-*San* gets on all fours to impersonate a hopping bunny-rabbit. The real bunnies respond with bunny-like movements without leaving their seats. A drunk Maeda-*San* pulls down at the bits of bunny fur. What happens next? Ten pairs of eyes slink across glass and slide along skin looking for breasts and then more. Several fingers cannot stay still. The once bunny-girl swishes the hair away from her face and removes the bunny wear from the other girl. Now standing, the nudes fondle one another and do a kind of dance. The penguins stay seated and stare, still and dumb, following the dance closely. After a while one man taps his small fingers on the table in time with the women's pump-pump. Everyone then taps his fingers on the table until the girl-girls stop dancing.

A video screen, inlayed in the mirrored wall begins to tingle and scratch as it receives its current. The image of a man sodomizing a woman appears on the wall. The couple is standing up to the waist in water. Their faces and shoulders are not visible, cut off from view by the wavy edge of the water's surface wriggling across the top of the screen.

His movements generate the waves.

To prevent her body from floating away, his rigid member must hold anchor. Her voice begs him not to stop. She fears the incoming tide.

There is a cut to the image of a nude unconscious woman beached at the edge of the shore and yet still whipped and rolled by the splattering waves as they reach the shore. Her long hair wraps in tangles across her face and neck. A close-up of her lips reveals a cut on the cheek. She is rolled onto her belly. The camera pans down her body and pauses at her buttocks. With the next crashing wave she is rolled again onto her back. Between her legs flows red and brown seaweed, out of which a crab appears and crawls toward her sand-encrusted pubis.

The video program continues with a more humorous clip at a sushi bar. Beside the other pieces of raw fish displayed behind the curved vitrine is a nude woman. Lying belly up, she appears slightly cramped in the sushi chef's well organized but small work area. Her bent knees are parted while her bare feet inch their way onto his wood chopping block. Quickly shifting the small group of shrimp and large clams aside, the sushi-chef selects a rectangular slab of tuna. His deft movements and sharp blade produce several pieces. Hands to the left and right swing a group of dishes onto his counter, fingers in the rice and a patting in his palm form five little beds. Before artfully arranging the bite-sized pieces on several pink porcelain dishes, he masturbates the woman with the little slivers of raw fish. Each dish is sculpted after a woman's body part. The heroic sushi chef serves his guests, who seem undisturbed in their male chatter by the woman's throaty moans and evermore swollen lips. The men seem to enjoy the food. They order more; one or two of them nod toward the chef to indicate his approval. After the meal is over, the sushi chef places

14

a deep cup in front of each man. Reflected in their clear green tea is the image of a net full of fish flung on a wood deck, tails flapping, bodies arching, and gills opening for air.

The head of a snoring penguin drops into the pillow of one of the bunny seats. Others are hungry, their hands foraging across the table for edible morsels.

The two women have long since disappeared, leaving behind their bunny-wear strewn across the table autographed on the inner lining. The hostess makes several trips to the table. She takes away used glasses, cleans the ashtrays and brings an arbitrary number of deep cups of green tea. At the bar she changes the videocassette. Later, she asks her guests to join her in a *karaoke* session. No one replies. Within another half hour, the accounting department leaves in twos and threes supporting collapsed co-workers by the shoulder.

With closed eyes he fingers the remnant from the previous night. A pair of white puffs is wound around his thumb and forefinger by a white elastic cord. Although burdened with a grotesque hangover, he is surrounded by a reassuring familiarity. At every turn, he faces one of six permanently assembled backgrounds that comprise his very small apartment. His apartment is so small that there is nothing left over once the required area for all the props pinned to the apartments perimeter are subtracted. There is no room here for spontaneity, domestic gymnastics or to invite a woman for an extended stay.

He is fully dressed. His face is pinched on one side by a line of dry spittle spanning his cheek. Spurred by an insistent image of a woman's wide hips, he carefully removes the feathery bonbons and examines them more closely. On the leatherlike inner lining he finds the name *Candy-mae* inscribed in red metallic ink. He unbuckles his belt and partially unbuttons his trousers. A dense feeling hammers against his temples. He is desperate for a drink. He takes the few heavy steps to the sink and opens his mouth directly on the faucet stream. The water washes away the nasty residue on his tongue and refreshes his eyes and face. He straightens up.

Had it been a bit warmer or a bit colder, Kang would have traveled to his parents' house. He was in the mood for a filling, cost free meal and effortless conversation. But the day's bland weather absorbed his already debilitated initiative to make consequential decisions. He satisfied himself by reviewing how such a visit was usually spent.

An Overheard

Voice of diminished virility from one who had fully exercised his power of seduction year after year, era to era, climate to climate, while weathering the years as son, father, husband, lover.

He still has a wily way with women. Stiffer and stiffer as the years run away from him for fear of coming to a rigid standstill—perhaps now, he simply needs an ever longer arc of time to exercise his art.

Real Estate

Lily wants to build a house on P.'s estate.

P. has already built three beautiful houses on his large property. Two of these are relatively small structures, while the third is middling to large.

Lily lives on a property that is part of a new estate. Its group of four houses is well planned and effectively coordinated.

Real estate is not all that attractive to Lily or P. but neither he nor she has avoided the business altogether.

In fact, if they travel together, they stay at hotels and tend not to concern themselves with the details of managing their respective estates.

P. needs to build a small shed to house his many tools. Because Lily is familiar with P.'s property, P. finds it useful to discuss his plans with her. As it is being built, the shed appears house-like. This continues to be the case even after all of P.'s tools are in place.

Lily wants to put up a tent on P.'s property. P. puts up no protest, but Lily doesn't follow through with her plans. "In my tent," she says, "I would always be anticipating impressions; I'd imagine a threat where there would actually be none—"

No one would understand her living in a tent and sleeping in a house.

Lily can always visit P.'s estate by bringing herself over in broad daylight. P.'s property is only deceptively large and uncultivated.

One fateful morning, Lily leaves all the windows of her house open. Wind blows through, gnawing at the walls. Various pieces break away and are blown to different positions in the house.

Lily leaves all the water faucets running. Her basins overflow. The floorboards, at first blackened and wet through, are soon looking up through a layer of water. Water stains creep up the papered walls.

She enters the kitchen. Much debris has landed on the stovetop. The flame from one of four burners is enough to raise hell.

Lily is already running to P.'s estate as the three other houses burst into flames.

She enters one of his houses, opens all the windows, the faucets, and her flame-throwing mouth.

The fire burns—Lily wakes up under the open sky inhaling the acrid smell of wet ashes deeply into her nose. Upon standing, she notices a stream crossing the property that she had overlooked before.

Lily walks along its edge. The walking brings her back to her property—she turns around and walks back to his. She continues walking back and forth, property to property, until she must finally sit down from exhaustion.

Her eyes relax on the water. She lets a hand dangle and cause a braid of ripples.

She feels for the slippery mud beneath the mat of leaves.

Today's Performance

She arrived at the table and sat down with her flavored gelatin dessert and mug of coffee. She had chosen the one with a dollop of cream. Pinned to the edge of her seat and leaning in towards flight, she spooned the food into her mouth with a rapid-fire delivery. Her concentration was so complete that she didn't notice the slightly older woman beside her reading her newspaper. The other woman read and chewed her food at the same time and most likely did not consider eating and reading at the same time especially difficult. By the time the dessert glass was scraped clean, the trembling woman received calls for an encore. Another dessert? Two spoons? Lower mouth directly into dish and lap it up, suck it in, lick it clean?

On My Way Home

I'm 21. Button-down blouse, tight fitting to a trim figure. Black jeans—black ankle boots, well polished. My perfume is Indian-rose, lightly applied. It's 4:50 p.m. and I'm on my way home. I enter the airport waiting room. There are no seats anywhere and few travelers. It seems more like an entry hall than waiting room. In one corner is a large newspaper and candy store. Its display fans out into the hall. Unlike most other airports I have been to, this one has thick walls with old-fashioned, deeply set paneled windows. I could be in a train station if not for the fact that I have come to catch a plane.

As I walk across the well polished floor, I'm stopped by a stocky man with dirty blond hair dressed in a workman's blue overalls. He asks to see my passport. I am skeptical. Who is this guy? He wears a bushy moustache on a large, round face. Objectively speaking, he is good-looking. He seems personable, carrying himself like the lastborn child of a big family. A picture comes to my mind of a family where the parents love all their children. He is certainly the youngest, cute and chubby as a child, trailing behind at least three other older siblings. I notice that he speaks mostly in monosyllables. Longer vocabulary, and those harder to pronounce, he breaks into manageable tidbits. This tendency reminds me of those people who have the habit of cutting their evening meal—steak, potatoes, and broccoli into little bite-sized pieces before they set to work in the business of eating.

Without giving in to his request, I ask the man for his identification. I tell him I will not comply before seeing it.

Putting on a very serious face he says he is not authorized to do so and, "Please Miss, let's not waste time." I still refuse to show him anything and insist that the whole thing is absurd.

I can't say he becomes actually angry, as he is the type who seems to accept almost everything. Finally he leans in real close toward me. He smells like chocolate donuts and coffee. Under his breadth, he softly whispers that this airport has been targeted for a terrorist attack.

" Miss, I'm an undercover cop,"

"Oh, really," I say with a cocky tone.

"Yes. We have a tip that this airport is one of the targets. We want to prevent anything from happening. We would appreciate your compliance, Miss."

He goes on to explain that our meeting should seem casual, like any between a man and a woman.

"Miss, don't you have a book in your bag—Go ahead and slip your passport between the covers and then hand the book to me, saying something like, 'You should really read this one, it is very entertaining'." He is speaking so quietly that the movement of his lips seems exaggerated for the amount of sound that reaches my ears.

I realize that I could miss my plane if I continue with this guy. I make one more mistrusting study of his face and decide 5 out of 10 he's for real.

Reluctantly, deep in my purse, I assemble the book/passport as he had asked and hand it to him, saying in a loud voice, "This book is really a piece of trash, but I think you would enjoy it."

He scans the blurbs on the back cover before carefully opening the book to where I had inserted the passport. With a nod of his head I see he is satisfied. Returning the book, he thanks me silently before walking back over to the bestseller rack in the newspaper stand.

I'm discovering this airport, locating shops, toilets, departures. I assemble my kind of functional diagram. As a traveler, I want to be on top of things. Avoid wasted movements, ungraceful sequences. Allow no hysteria.

At the far left-hand corner of the room is the bridge to all gates. It is well lit by a horizontal band of high sidelights. The women's restroom is directly adjacent to the bridge. I turn in the direction of the undercover policeman before entering. He has already approached another woman. The whole procedure seems too out in the open to work successfully as an 'undercover operation.' But thinking it over, I realize that I enjoyed the whole scene—especially how my feigned indignation disturbed the sweet doughboy policeman.

I check my watch. I still have over half an hour before my flight. I take my time, holding my head in my hands as I sit on the toilet, letting each thought reach its fullest potential before moving on to the next. Later, I stare at my face in the mirror, opening the faucet to full and letting a powerful stream of water rush over my hands. I brush the top edge of my cheekbones with wet, ice-cold fingertips and linger over my image, thinking with a degree of satisfaction of the good impression I will make on my welcoming family.

I pass through the door and shiver when I feel a bony little hand cover my mouth. Since I also feel something hard pressed into the small of my back, I don't resist as the hands push me in the direction of the men's room. The hands shove my body against the door. It smoothly swings open and then closes behind us.

It feels very strange to witness a horrific scene with someone else's hand held over my mouth. My frantic breath and uncontrollable saliva coat the hand's palm and fingers as my disbelieving eyes take in the gruesome view. The bright light is harsh, reflected on all sides by the glossy white tiles. Of the four stalls, the doors of three are wedged open by three male corpses, collapsed on the floor, one with his trousers gathered at the ankles.

I feel a scream bursting its way through my eardrums when the hand falls away from my mouth. A female voice orders me to slowly turn around.

"Have you made yourself all prettied up for the flight?" As I am basically in a state of shock, I cannot feel certain she is actually speaking to me. She is an Asian woman. I guess perhaps Korean. She comes extremely close to me. She is examining me, touching me with her eyes. Perhaps now convinced of my physical weakness, she relaxes the arm holding the gun, letting it drop to her side. With her left hand she strokes my hair.

"It has been so long since I've had one as pretty as you." She spits onto her fingertips and then brings her hand under my shirt, pressing my nipples with her sticky fingers. A startling current runs through my body, grounding my feet firmly to the floor.

"Undress," she shrieks, her voice hoarse and complicated. With trembling fingers I slowly do as she says. My slowness is not intentional. The enormous effort required to force my body to move and correctly perform any action is overwhelming. She orders me to sit on the edge of the sink, my legs spread and wedged against the mirrored wall. She turns the faucet on full blast and directs the stream over my swelling lips.

"Hey bitch," she cries, "let me know when you are ice cold. Cold like ice, hard as ice, and fragile as ice." I don't say anything, as it is my jaw that feels frozen shut. She stops the water and touches me with her fingers.

"Ooh, aren't you a hot ice queen!" she says, pushing at my hips to shift me off the narrow shelf.

She takes off her heavy leather jacket and lays it on the tiled floor, indicating with her gun that I should lie on top. I feel as though I am made of fragile plaster: a hollow plaster cast with blood at its core. She empties one bullet from her gun onto the palm of her hand. With pincerlike fingers she picks it out and inserts it in my mouth. I cannot help myself from actively sucking on it as if it were a hard candy, pressed down and rolled back and forth between tongue and palette.

She removes her shirt and slides her fingers down my body, rubbing my genitals until the hole is wet and the lips swollen. With wetted fingers she rubs the barrel of her gun before slipping over a rubber sheath. She directs the gun at my breasts saying, "Pow! Pow, pow!" I shrink back instinctively and let out a pitiful scream. By the time she has the gun in me, bringing it repeatedly in and out, I can no longer think. I am in an almost ecstatic state, a horrifying mixture of terror and arousal. She is on her knees bouncing up and down like a baby, her little breasts bobbing wildly.

Without warning she slips it out and lays it on the tiled floor beside my head.

I slowly recover the pair of soft wet balls set in the bone-framed sockets of my skull. I sense them strain to register any visual information. The fine perforation of the ceiling's acoustic panels, the chrome-colored gridwork blocking a direct view of the flourescent tubes, the smooth glossiness of the toilet stall partitions. I follow the generous curve of the toilet's underside, and the sculpted appearance of a blood-soaked shirt. Here and there, red fluid has made its way along the recessed grooves between the white ceramic tiles.

My eyes are fingering their way through the full head of hair that interrupts my view to the left. I'm terrified to realize that I am taking control of my own head, rolling it to the left and to the right. This self-consciousness moves along muscle and limb making my skin taut. I become painfully aware of the gaping hole that was only moments before tucked safely away clothed and protected. I roll my head to the right and her compact, small figure is in view.

Out of my discarded shirt she rips a washcloth-sized piece of cloth, retrieves the gun and orders me to my hands and knees. When I do so she shrieks happily and thrusts my buttocks high in the air. I feel her lay the gun down at the small of my back. Her eyes are glued to me as she shuttles backward to the sink. I cannot see what she is doing there and even wait for her return. She is cleaning me, wiping my anus with the wet cloth as if I were a helpless baby. She kneels in front of my face and folds the cloth in four. She gently wipes my brow before stuffing the cloth into her own pocket. She is so close; I can smell her rancid sweat.

"Since they are still here" she spits out, "I think you should get a special treat!" She charges at one of the corpses and extends an arm flat across the floor. Pressing down firmly on the palm, she cuts off the middle finger with a switchblade retrieved from inside her clothes. I try to close my eyes and open them again, as if to banish my participation in an impossible nightmare. My eyes fall closed again as I feel the finger press its way into me, and then her gun . . . I hear my voice rhythmically drawing more of her over me. It hooks her attention as it does mine. My movement draws her in more deeply, incorporating her active parts as part of what I am becoming. I visualize all her tools, to better amplify her proficiency in employing them to my benefit. The gun's knobs pressing through the rubber sheath, sharpening her contact to my inner skin, they trace and retrace the ever-denser web of my responsiveness.

The detached finger is no longer grotesque. It behaves now as it should: a man's thick finger, animating and expanding the circumference of my pleasure. If her action changes, I am no longer aware of the shifts in her attentions. I sense only my body's enclosure stretching beyond recognition and sucking back at itself blindly.

I do hear her voice. It is ordering me to stand and to dress. Something has ended and the dread returns. My clothes no longer feel like my own. I am afraid they will not fit my huge body. If I feel any pain, I am no longer able to locate it or to care. Is she speaking to me? I try to focus on her mouth, and then her hands . . . and the gun? Stunned, I apply myself to the task of buttoning my shirt. My skin is marked by large red blotches that the ripped shirt will no longer hide. I am pushed out into the main hall.

She holds the gun to my neck. My jaw is cramped and sore from the effort not to swallow the bullet. Creeping down along the side of my face, all my attention is directed at the gun's position, to pinpoint its contact with my skin, to envelop its shaft, and freeze the trigger. I want to convince myself that the gun is more part of me than it is her weapon. The moment arrives and my hands reach up, grip and push downward with all the force I can gather. Perhaps simply from surprise she doesn't shoot, and loses the gun. I swing at her head and then again and again, each time releasing a compressed shot of air.

I hear her moans, and she crumples to the ground, to an eerie silence. I can barely look at her now. I want not to know how much I have hurt her. It is only a fleeting image of completion that brings me to my senses. I gather my remaining strength and drag her limp body through the bathroom door and then deeper into the middle stall. I lock the door and crawl out fully aware that my efforts to imprison her will be ineffectual.

Preoccupied by the thought that I still possess her gun, this obsession precludes all else. I open a large window with the intention to throw the gun down to the courtyard below. A fixed screen blocks the way. I am almost in hysterics and start to swing at the screen with the gun. It goes off, the shot resounding in the empty hall. I am unsure in which direction the bullet was fired and quickly scan the room for any apparent damage. The screen remains intact. Below, I see the bare concrete courtyard. It seems to be asking for the gun. But after several repeated attempts to puncture the screen, I give up, drop the gun to the floor and run out of the airport.

Something happened I wouldn't have imagined. If I hadn't been on my way home I might have been looking for something. I would have set the stakes for that adventure I believed I should have.

Now, wherever I stand, things take sides. My body is polarized into familiar and unfamiliar regions. Can I say or should I announce that certain of these impatiently await identification as regions? Then at times I sense this group or another begging for a revisitation. I even make plans. I tell myself that in order to lead a full life, I should hypostatize contradictions as I encounter them, at the very least when I believe them to exist.

I do seem frightened. "How am I different from that Korean woman?" I asked myself yesterday as I stood beneath the showerhead—and if the event had never actually happened—it's not the kind of thing you would go around trying to verify.

The other day I read in the papers how a writer who had written a novelized memoir of his childhood in Auschwitz is being accused of fraud. They say he was born too late, to non-Jewish parents, etc. In short, that he made the whole thing up. Without doubt, the story required much research to construct. Supposedly tainted with imposture, it was severely examined and criticized for minor inaccuracies. The author was attacked for misrepresenting himself. But can't we say he wrote the story for those who were not able to do so—as proof that you can put yourself into someone else's shoes if you really want to? Why would even the authentic victim write such a book if not, at least in part, to test the limits of empathy?

But the undeniable thing is that I consider myself lucky that this whole thing happened. This is my story. And then I do know that I never actually made it there. To my parent's house.

The Appointment

"Set yourself here. Yes."

"Your arms—should go back there. That's right. Do you feel the handle? Do you feel that thing sticking out? There are four holes for your fingers, and your thumb wraps around—Yes, that's right. Good. How does it feel? Not too tight? Not too uncomfortable? Now, let's go to the feet—no, maybe we should do the hips first—you might need to use your legs to push up.

O.K. I want you to slide up to here—no, a bit higher. Hmm, let me see here—if I can lift—Now you. O.K. we got it. Are you all right?

This whole thing should slide back and forth—see if you can get it to move—yes. I'm not sure, try a combination of your arms and hips. Your legs won't move—so I think you'll have to use your arms. Yes, that's it. O.K. let's tie the feet down. This one is simple. You don't have to do anything.

Now I'm going to go out and turn down the lights and come back though the other door. You won't be able to see me, but you'll hear me, I'm sure.

O.K. Last check. Hands, back, bottom, feet—good.

—be back soon!"

Door. He said door. Wait for the sound of it. Blanketed with the idiocy of agreeing to stage directions—to specific cues. Door click: a needle-fine pop. Self-conscious effort enters. Eyes open staring at that self-conscious approach.

Sweating right at the small of the back, at the crease between thigh and groin, at the temples, the forehead, back of head, the corner of eyes.

I don't really know what it is, regardless. Irregardless, it's a color and in the color is a stalker (with feet, legs). Feet that slap the floor, and then more, muted, the stage—poked, pressed, un-met and un-touchable. He's pulling up and the piece slides in its track bringing the appointed closer to a large mouth. Tools like fingers peel open the blunt cap's growing fruit. An already wet mouth licks the juices. Cart falls back: knees knock together. Again, pulled back up, still on track. Knees fall apart. Flaps around the hole rolled back open—licked—liked—sweaty bottom slides a bit. Errant grunt. Errant muscle lengthened. Tendency stretched into pointed tent. Here come the grunting elephants! I don't like it! Slide and wriggle. Disgust wriggles in. Disgust incorporated. Disgust celebrated! Elephants shrink behind paired tent flaps.

Through double grunt. Collapse and retreat behind double grunt.

Speaking easier now: talking to the voided stage of willed movement.

Who cares that it works. Its force immense? No. My recoil, successful? No. The piece slid in its tracks. The room was focused.

Settled in the armchair. Come sit in my lap.

The woman who sits in the lap abdicates her own throne of dissent, of argumentation, of proposition. She has followed the lead to reposition and repeat: to repeat herself, otherwise.

Then, however, there is the open book posture. "Read me," she says. "What am I that sits spine in hold, frontally splayed?"

Leila's Friends

She is a child of 23 who wants to make worldly ripples in the big sea. Leila is familiar enough with geography to say: the Mediterranean Sea is lukewarm and has a gentle surf, and innocent enough to believe that the Arabian, the Black and the Caribbean Seas are too far away to influence her currently.

She paints herself with waxy reds to attend an adult party at the house of family friends—without her parents. Luckily, there beside an empty shelf, she meets Maxwell, historian of heroic undertows, Gulfstreams and vibrating Gibralters. Leila articulates her ambitions bringing her willingness to the fore. It's necessary, she says and points his attention to her young lips, the victory pattern of her dress and her strong thighs.

Maxwell Abraham, also four times the father, questions Leila's degree of achievement and depth of daring and suggests that her erotic posturing reveal the amateur.

Have you any idea what sacrifices some have made, my darling girl? It's never mere costume nor masquerade. There is no risk here, no daring game—though I'm glad to be privy to your earnest try. How will you continue, you need to ask, are you prepared for an initiate's initial task?

He whispers the florid details pertaining to an Egyptian ritual into Leila's swelling face. He blows the words into her ears and against her cheeks—as soft lashings—as if to protect the sanctity of his narrative against contamination by its drifting too far afield over living room furniture.

. . . The ceremony begins at sunset. A herd of young virgins are bustled to the banks and bound by the wrists to the back ends of wide ceremonial rafts. The women are swaddled in carefully dyed cloth and towed up river by a rapidly rowing team of slaves. Several numbing hours pass before their floating train is assaulted by muscular figures who swim up to the rafts and repeatedly attack the young women with their brightly painted bodies and twisted sticks. The men swim over and under them, over and under until the cloth releases its pigment into the river water. When the sun rises the

rafts can be seen slowly advancing up river, trailed by a wide band of red-colored water.

Some are quickly lost. They drown, deaf to the call to raise their heads for a mouthful of air. As if becoming ritual vessels their mouths are frozen open to the rush of the river's flow. Others, trained from an early age to withstand hours in the muddy river, their taut wiggling bodies smeared with thick layers of animal fat, survive the grueling ceremony with an athletic endurance.

But, the important point, says Maxwell, *is that they are faceless. This ritual is not a performance. The women receive no reward for their participation. Nevertheless, they constitute something essential. They play their part in the confrontation of unrestrained movement with the inertia of domestic settlement. The women are never brought back to shore. Kept in the middle of the river by hedges of canoes, their bodies are untied and released into the water's flow. After enduring 24 hours in the water not a single woman is able to swim to dry land. One interesting practice, not strictly part of the significance of this yearly rite, is that the women are given strong hallucinogens before being tied to the rafts. They therefore experience their actual fate only elliptically . . . perhaps appropriately so.*

Maxwell knocks the remaining gritty wine from the glass into his resonant mouth and tenderly touches Leila's cheek.

. . . Good wine and the tragic figure of a beautiful woman . . .

With this last remark he walks over to the sofa where his big-breasted wife is smoking the life out of a cigarette. He sits down beside her, placing his hand on her thigh. Not wishing to overhear their conversation, Leila leaves the party earlier than expected feeling dizzy and uncomfortably queasy.

Shuttling between night and day, art and labor, silence and mutability, Leila rides her train homeward. Within a swaying crowd she cocks her head to read the face of a scholarly beard.

. . . he looks like a Marxist. He reads philosophical books. He is un-ironed, woolen, and full of well chewed words. He must be a tree of knowledge: he is holding a Kabbalic text . . . Why not?

His fingers, drawn across the page, are intent on receiving. He brings one long finger to his lips to moisten its tip to turn the page. Leila does the same; all of this is enough to give way to her curiosity to wish to know what he would say to a girl who'll peel off his corduroy jacket, obviously interested in a naked spine. He, with heavy satchel and full with beard and she, parasitic to the root, disband the train. They stop for a cup of tea. Leila is brimming over with vulgarity, but declines a danish, silently chanting, *I will not eat inedibles, inedibles, inedibles.*

To her surprise, in his well kept home he is cordial and affably casual. They share a bowl of popcorn and he promises a bedtime story. As Leila prematurely confirms, this bibliophile seems to attract strange episodes. The tales begin as a matter of fact. Once upon a time there was a woman who cried to be sprayed with whipped cream. Being a gentlemanly lover he consented to her wish for cover; he described her panting as she lay on the table while he transformed her into a monotonous meal. Cream and sex, nipples and hollows, endlessly melting, sticky drops landing on the floor . . . another dash to the grocery store.

Then he introduced Lorraine, a come-to-life comic strip babe. She entered his room, sat on his sofa, and made herself his meal. She rolled out of her clothing: suction-pop, suction pop-pop and mounted the beard with thighs. The action developing with her galloping hips froze a few frames later; just long enough for Lorraine to communicate her need—an ecstatic phrase trapped in a bubble. Balloons! Balloons between my body and yours. Pop them darling! When I reach for the stars! It only took several pricks of a pin, he said with a chuckle. And Leila, always the child, never exactly knowing what is expected of her, kept vigil in her sweaty sleeping bag beside the scholar's bed the entire night long, smothering any fantasy that might show its little head. When morning broke, she refused a full egg breakfast and walked the long way home.

Late evening, a few weeks later, sidewalk friendly Leila bumps into a new boundary. Seeking a not unattractive incidental anyman with whom to couple, she spots a possible post and follows him around the bend.

Both easy prey, attentive to such cat and mouse, the two scurry up the stairs of her parents' house. He paws and he scratches and he even bites. She wiggles and tingles, her eyes seemingly bright. He begins with his calculated entry that transmogrifies into the calibrated attack. Dialogue superfluous, he probes her prettiness by slapping her thigh and her meatiness by pinching her mini-buds. When flowers to be, if flowers must be and if, when, how long, how big? Whole flowers in waiting: many, many of them . . .

Don't you like a smart slap? I do and I don't and in the end I won't but I'll let you for now until I put up a fight.

They meet once again—there is a modicum and flicker of fun, but there's also a bad smell somewhere Leila can't put her finger on.

The next time he rents a hospital bed, prepared with starched and spotless sheets. He and she rub the cloth until it's noticeably soft and natural. Morning arrives, and as they leave the borrowed room, Leila turns her head and snaps up a postcard picture of the sun-sharpened outlines of the rumpled sheets piled on top of the bed for later on.

The last time, in transit to the Capitol, he calls to make arrangements. Facing her calmly, late afternoon, he unzips his case and justly pulls out the handcuffs. He is part of a club, yes, *there are many of us. We know what we are doing, we abide by our rules . . . there's really no harm to it—come, I'll fix you to the bed—please trust me.* She holds herself back. She won't go any further. She can't muster the desire for this registered professional.

Throughout the next months, the questions invaded her house. They taunted her with lascivious whistling through unguarded holes. Loudly!—inscribing their patterns and playing a catchy tune— Loudly! Nesting in clumps behind sensitive membranes, it was easy for one to wiggle free from its neighbors and spring open to strike the taut drum. Can you imagine your body's ambition? How often and to what end? Who? Who! Pantheon or constellation? Haven't the painfully pointed entries left a scour of scars? And what have you learned? And has it already reached—will it be ugly—or so sudden that you would cry for joy?

The questions, rhythmic knocks, and clever twisters understood Leila's convoluted anatomy and were able to crawl right through to meet and contrive the idea for the next forage. Participating organs contracting to the question's orchestration of her evolving body— (as would the others). And if others: anonymous, classified! Collaborating participants in the hypothesis. *Who eggs me on? My well-being swells—I might soon be conscious fodder. But for what? With whom?* The door latch clicks shut. There flowing in a row: beads or balls of flesh with hair sprouting from their heads. Her knees march toward the traffic. As if by recipe, she skims the surface of the bubbling soup to taste the rising scum. The questions had once again crowded out her loneliness.

Once and Again

When he strikes I become numb. I see the area of our contact as separate from myself: colorful, unusual and inattentive to my directions.

For example, I had my legs wide open—there was some sort of loud obnoxious party going on: happenings on the floors the walls (and below the exposed electric wiring), and a red glow blanketed everything.

It must have been the red glow that blocked the important dialogue between demonstrative puppets posturing there after the curtain had been pulled back. For me, what was missing in this performance were the strings to the puppets' smallest parts, which take just as long to learn to operate as to attach.

The Knoll

I noticed that she pulled away from him slightly, holding back the usual chorus of adoring caresses and kisses. She resisted the pressure from his hand on her head that pushed her towards his central root of pleasure—club of power.

I heard her whisper: I want to stay above the surface, above hatred and rejection and slide away from adoration and disturb the advance of blind devotion . . . I lie open as a landscape, knobbed and rutted, grassy and cool . . .

But he wanes, unhinged from his own physical gravity—here confused, still flailing in another place.

        I, more voluptuous.
        You, less realized.

        You, body to be adored
        I, the worshiper.

        I, hanging from a wire above an opening
        You, below looking up into the opening
        I, unfolding
        You, entering.

Officer P

I.

The law officer makes his way across the maze, way ahead of the effects that may be caused by his penetrating search of the perpetrator of the crime. He is undaunted by any crime, this crime, for example, nor by what will soon be his own. This law officer is never alone. But he, in her midst, is not alone in desiring the stage for himself or in desiring the female curl of the woman dancing on the stage. Drinking much too much, he engulfs the stage blinding another to her closing call. The female curl, smooth and compliant lacks an instinctual resistance to bodily assault. Performing is in her a purely vibratory pose as if she were purely vibratory. Rarely, if at all, pausing to contract, as if her musculature were no longer intact, she withstands reform. Eventually deformed by the exhumed officer's blows as he battles, staging the battle of his own judicial process against self in self-incrimination, redoubling his attempts to kill her before he destroys himself.

Hooked by the skin loosened in the brawl he is pulled free from this tentesticled entrapment; still drunk, blood poisoned, won't he now be of little use in law enforcement?

II.

Officer P had a cavernous capacity
to drink himself silly.
Round in the roll, strapped as a barrel
Filled to his lids with occupational hatreds
His hands became hotter
His pulse, a hammer
To pummel the dancer
He pulled off from the stage

Fixed into place, eyes in his pockets,
He aims and he shudders
and explodes in her socket.
P's shot full of holes
He's torn and he's leaking
His transgression pooling
Inexcusably exposed

Now she is finished—
there are shreds everywhere . . .

Officer P lost his case
There is nothing left but this indented carapace.

III.

So P opens the door to the Black Rose and walks right in. He wants to see the proprietress. He sits down, gets a drink, and she comes out to show him her properties. This joint is something of a cave. I've already described what happens in the cave, but to quickly recount— P's belly is uncompromisingly convex. When he gets into a fight about whose performance is whose, he crowds out the other claimant with his sheer volume.

P and his prize, Miss Blond, leave through the private rear exit, the cave's anus, which opens out onto an uncharted sea. There is the boat: a simple shell with no rigging. P stands in the prow, erect and stalwart. The curl swoons and finds her place on the rear seat. She is wrapped in fur, her bleached face framed in a blond curl.

There is just enough boat to convey the statuesque figures through the stylized waves profiled in white foam, and just enough boat to prevent the couple from slipping off the skiff as the boat responds to the sea's shocks and jolts.

The two figures, the black and the blond, the rigid and the supple, the weapon wielding aggressor and the yielding open question approach the rock island. The island, like the waves into which it is set, is also a carefully profiled element, jagged and well textured.

From the beginning, she was co-opted. The employee: the well-dressed violation of her bodily property: costumed, managed and drunkenly swaying between performed perfection and irreducible captivity. P extinguishes her, never recognizing her incomplete complicity in his own crime. Dead, but already eddying into standard Venus molecules—she is loved but destroyed, extracted, ground into powder, applied, inserted and discovered impregnating feminine thresholds. Moments later, years after, eons even, all the while eddying into standard Venus molecules, she will once again develop organs: a functioning vagina, full breasts, and a head of flowing hair.

Untitled

(Someone is speaking French—is she speaking to me? Sh! How beautiful—I love that voice.

It's a melody. No, it's not a melody. It's an explanation. She's telling us what we should do—what everyone does to receive the service. Listen—hear that? There, she said it again: the same thing. She wants me to put all my valuables in that jar. Tick, tick . . . she's pointing to her wrist: my watch. Yes, and my chain. She's telling me to undress—to empty my pockets. Look, she is checking—Ha! She doesn't trust me. She thinks I am hiding something. She's even checking the lining for irregularities. She runs the back of her nails across my skin. She tells me to bend over—This is too much—She's checking between my legs—For what? . . . a pin, a chain, a cock ring? She pushes down on my back. She wants me to submit. She sticks a finger up my ass—certainly not to please me. She's feeling for something: the word in German is *tasten*: feeling, checking, tapping all in one movement.

What's that? She's wearing a mechanical cock: a drill. She's breaking ground—looking for a pellet of gold, a satchel of drugs, encrusted jewels. Can you imagine: this French-speaking whore searching up my ass? And just to prove that her action makes good sense, like a magician, she even finds what she claims to be looking for. Between two thickly enameled nails she holds up a chiseled garnet to the light. She says: *c'est ça*, with that all-knowing French finality. How could I not know myself? The thought makes me blow soap bubbles and my rear starts to throb: it's trying to tell me something; maybe there is a lot more there—another precious stone, a gold mine. She knew it. They all do: it's so logical. I might just be a rich man! I say *encore*, *encore* . . . or *alors* . . . or something else I know she will understand as French).

The Woman

The pulse held diagonally in the muscular wrap of her throat is unusually prominent. It could be a signal. I'm quite worried. What will happen next? There are many things in the room that are in the wrong place. A large pile of unfolded clothes covers the couch. She's repeating the names of things and taking a look around, at times crooning her neck to target the right place. There are crumbs under the table and hairy dust collected around the standing lamp. Then there's the mess of her own body still cradled in the chair. She wants something better than gratuitous help. I change the pitch of my voice—something I've taught myself to do—with a swell melodic line I come out of the corner. My eyes meet hers in just the right way to ease her tension. It's the timbre of my voice, the way the rising pitch suggests elevation—a rising hopeful feeling. She's eased. Her pulse recedes. And the room's walls blend once again into an even background. She'll remember the rise: the swell meeting and pressing into her—I'm sure of it. So I send her a gratuitous smile and disappear.

She Twists to Position Her Face

She twists to position her face supported by her entire heavy upper body into the scene. What leads her face? The eyes? But not in isolation. It is something with more skin and more point. Undereye and nose—a complex skin kinship—presses into an existing cluster of faces: into their conversation.

That prodding thing. That thing she's using to get in, she points it toward the center. Good old Mary never has been able to get in, to the center, to the inner circle for which every bit of content is interdependent, conscious of its correct participation and its value—in this best of configurations. She has to use this pointed part of herself to break in, uninvited, to make an opening for her big body and big self to join the circle. She is blond. True gold.

Mary sat idle in a low-slung beach chair staring at a patch of white daisies at the edge of the pond. Finally she got up, walked over and picked one of the flowers that was bent away from the rest and returned to her seat. The yellow hill fills the middle. Pull a petal out—the others tremble. The gold mound will fill the picture. Mary plucked petals from the picked daisy.

Edged by trees and bushes sufficiently dense to give the feeling of a boundary, the large expanses of well-tended lawn flanked the paved asphalt path that led to the lake. On one side of the path the lawn rose steeply up to the small building that housed the changing rooms and showers. Below, on the other side of the path, the lawn buckled into a low linear berm before spreading out into a flat area. Beyond this, the ground fell again sloping into a very shallow paved depression filled with water. The grassy areas surrounded a large lake, a small portion of which was cordoned off for swimming.

Lying on the grass in Taghkanic State Park: a woman with her two children: a woman with her husband and two children.

The absence here of house walls and operable windows makes for an open display of relations. But really, here, out in the open landscape, the only thing I was concerned to show and with the proper care was my body, partially clothed, and its desire for physical communion, not necessarily with another but with the sensuality of the body itself. It was earlier in the morning as I was turning the large sheets of my newspaper against the sky when I first heard her loud, intrusive voice. She barged into the park with three children.

The two boys appeared first with a sure and confident advance across the lawn. Although their bodies fell and rose with the ground they seemed oblivious.

One blew moist air through his loose lips and shot out his hand to dramatize how his body would enter the water. The other boy dropped himself more vertically and almost soundlessly into the water. He used his whole arm to describe his movement. This must have been the way they prepared themselves. It was only mid-morning and the water would still be quite cold.

Mary marched along the crest of the berm, yelling directions. She was burdened with towels, a folded-up lawn chair and a few brightly colored plastic toys. Mary turned her head as she walked: cheeks and shoulder muscles flexing, breathy snorts forced out of her nose. Her body and her voice gave one the sense of an unavoidable heaviness, which despite her sometimes sharp and sudden movements, was difficult to dispel. She saw me look up and spoke out loudly, not directly to me, but to an unspecified extended audience.

"It's only when their holiday is over that I finally get to take a vacation. These kids are running me ragged. They want to go everywhere and I have to go along." She hiked on, vigorously, found a good position from which to watch the children and dropped her load.

Having realized that I had been staring directly at her, I unbuttoned my shirt and stretched my arms in back of my head. I inhaled the warm breath of summer. The cut grass had yet to be raked and clung between my toes.

The third child, a little girl, kept a distance between herself and the boys and a different distance from Mary. She was in a trance finding her way through blades of grass, taking note of the dense bushes, the fallen twigs, and seizing upon two red and white striped straws that had been left behind.

Mary restlessly watched the boys dive into the water. She sat surrounded by the children's things: three towels, their clothes, a Frisbee, and a large cloth bag with the insignia of a church organization. She did not pull out a book or a magazine and simultaneously appeared nervous and distracted.

The inner white lining of a pair of shorts formed a small tent on top of a red T-shirt. Mary grabbed the clothes, folding and stacking them into a sloppy pile. She rubbed her lower shin and ankle. Something close to the joint. She rubbed a bit more. I followed her movements, wanting to hear that unpleasant penetrating voice again. She sat on a large towel but it appeared as if she were sitting in her own property: a pig in mud, the yolk in the white of the egg.

Six shoes pointed in all directions. One pointed towards the girl. Mary watched as the girl, kneeling on her slender knees, pivoted around on the ball of one foot to tend to her work and continue her monologue. Her movements were efficient and elegantly deliberate. By screwing them into the ground, she had turned the straws into vertical posts. Using small piles of plucked grass she made a small ritual encampment. Mary walked to the edge of the lake. I repeatedly heard the exasperated voice call out: "Steve, Jesse! Time to come out of that water!"

The sun had risen over the trees and hit the floating white platform. The two boys' heads and glistening bodies repeatedly popped out of the water as they hoisted themselves up to the platform. Their firm bodies were never still—a restless athleticism expressed itself in their physically fluent communication. Steve jumped down then up and stretched his arms, entering the water as a taut bow. Jesse tested the springiness of the anchored raft. He jumped high and simply entered the water feet first.

The girl looked up to watch as a group of four figures approached the park. The small people were at that moment just the right size to enter her grass church without knocking over the red and white posts.

Three of them carried lawn chairs and one or two shopping bags. One held a chubby little girl's hand. They arrived at a generous flat area a short distance from the kiddy pool and dropped their things.

One yelled over to Mary, "We've brought lunch—Where are the boys?"

Mary answered also yelling, " In the water. I've been calling them but they won't come out."

The colored abundance spread out on the lawn. The chairs were positioned one, two, three in a semi circle, and the three adults settled down. The pudgy little girl ran over to the girl in the grass to see what she had made. The seated one continued to work, elbowing the air with her bony arms and making every effort to ignore the other's interest.

The elders bore no resemblance to the children; but the homogeneity of the three middle-aged guardians was uncanny. The smooth-faced man had something effeminate about him. The concavity in his cheeks, the warmth in his eyes, the relative paucity of forehead furrows seemed to foreshadow a future as a gradually emerging woman. His companions: his sisters, his colleagues—his shifting mirrors in their thick wooden bodies with squared faces and short cut hair knocked shoulders and knees in light, jovial conversation.

The three sewed themselves into the canvas slings of the portable lawn chairs. Braiding their forearms, one woman slipped a cracker into her neighbor's mouth; she brushed the crumbs off her friend's inert chest; Oh! Did you see that bird! Reaching, arm over arm, naturally, at ease, across one another, back and forth: the late morning developed into early afternoon.

One of my children appeared, her face flat and large against the blue sky. I pulled her down on top of me, flirting in an intimate way. I squeezed her body. I sniffed her skin.

"You smell like grass, is that what you have been eating?"

"No Mama! I didn't eat grass."

"Yes, you chewed some grass, it's right in here," I said, tickling her belly.

I placed my sculpted cheek next to the full puffy softness of hers.

"Mmm, what a soft face you have. You must be a peach."

"But Mama, I'm not a peach."

"I'm hungry, are you hungry?"

My daughter nodded. "What do we have?"

"Peanut butter sandwiches, ham sandwiches or a hard boiled egg. What do you want?"

"Ham . . . and something to drink."

Despite myself, mother slipped into action and that sweet intimacy slipped away. I dug into the bag, pushing aside a damp towel and a ruffled book to retrieve the food containers. I lay them out and removed the covers. My nose was assaulted by the smell of boiled egg. Husband and son arrived and for the next fifteen minutes all of us fought over, chewed up and swallowed the food. Afterwards he and I picked at the remains. As he was sweeping away the last potato chips from the corner of the plastic box, I was wishing our picnic props, my husband and our children would also be wiped from view.

While they planned a further outing, I busied myself at the border and later helped with their preparations. I tried to be patient as they prepared to leave; I tried not to appear too happy. I cleared away the lunch. After collecting and depositing the last bits of food and ripped wrappers, I snapped the plastic containers shut. I shook out the picnic towel and folded, rolled and returned it to the canvas travel bag. I packed a drink and snack for their outing. Finally I prepared a warm goodbye, see you later and have fun, and saw them off with two hugs and the tip of a kiss.

Left alone—children out of earshot, husband gone. Those well matured, intimate references packed away and gone.

I tried to see myself as if from a great distance: the image of a body holding a pose on the gentle grassy slope, midway between paved path and shallow water basin. I thought this view of myself could be attractive; I moved in closer—checked if I really was desirable; I hovered over abdomen, up legs bent at the knees and swaying to the side, not pushed by the wind but according to a shifting inner current of awakened arousal. The grass again, the prickly grass. Spread out on the ground—splayed out on the grass. As I heard those conversations, I lay on the grass, acutely conscious of the prickly sensations along my legs and the small of my back.

Mary arrived, her urgency and her discomfort, presumably caused by the heat, plainly legible in her face. She pulled groceries from the bags making several disapproving gestures. As if she were the only responsible person in the group with sweaty determination she began preparing the lunch.

The pudgy girl inched her way back to the large checkered picnic blanket dragging her feet and the cloth with it. Stepping between bags of potato chips, bottles of soda, a stack of ham, pickles and mayonnaise, she squatted on the only free area of cloth. Mary looked up, and in a voice incongruous with her facial expression, spoke to the girl.

"How's my little Lucy? You like it here, don't you?"

Without answering, the girl poked repeatedly at the potato chip bag with a rigid pointer finger.

"You want some?"

The girl nodded. Mary pulled open the bag and offered it to her. The girl's hand pounced into the bag and pulled out a sandy fistful. A triumphant smile broke across her face as she munched on the chips.

"Can't you speak any more?"

The girl shook her head vigorously and laughed, sending a small flock of chip bits flying onto Mary's thigh.

"How about your shoes? Where are they? I told you I don't want you going barefoot around here. There's glass on the road that can cut your foot. So go get them on, now!"

A little hand quietly slipped out another couple of chips and popped them into her mouth. The round faced little girl stood up, laughing, and dashed away.

The boys, Steve and Jesse, arrived carrying with them the chill, fresh wetness of the lake. They were excited: their movement jerky and manic because of the cold.

Another young couple arrived with a baby. Bill, smiling, walked toward them and helped carry over their things.

Everyone found a place around the picnic blanket.

Mary had opened the package of sliced bread and began preparing sandwiches. Shaking her head, one of the seated women called over to her, "No, Mary, don't do that. Everyone can prepare his own. Just make one for yourself. Each of us likes it his own way. I like only cheese, no meat, with lettuce and mayonnaise; Bill takes his with mustard, ham and pickles—and, how about you, David?" The woman was smiling, obviously pleased with herself, she looked around and continued, "Only David will eat anything." She broke into a laugh, walked over and hugged David from behind, leaning her greying head into the crook of his neck, "Mmm, I just love you. You're so good."

Mary covered the open face with a mayonnaise smeared slice and without turning toward the woman began muttering,

"I know what the kids like. I make them lunch every day. But if you don't want me to do anything, I won't." Dropping the knife onto the blanket, Mary took one of the sandwiches and rose to her feet. She shook her head more vigorously and sat down with a heavy plop at the far corner of the blanket. She began immediately to eat her food and had already finished her sandwich before the others had even begun. She repeatedly assumed a distraught face, made short shakes of the head and clicked her tongue.

From where I lay, I saw the backs of the young couple. The parents, Rachel, and David and baby Louisa occupied an entire side of the blanket. Eating was clearly very important for all three of them. They let everyone else know just how important it was. What, how much, and how heartily the mother Rachel ate was addressed by Rachel herself by both of the older women and by David, the father. Although Rachel accepted David's participation in the preparation of her food, Rachel wanted to feed herself. She monitored the speed and quantity of her intake. She even overplayed it as a kind of performance. She says, grinning, "What an appetite! I can't stop! I never used to eat like this!" She laughed pretending to be surprised at her voraciousness. They kissed one another, and crossed arms as one or the other reached for more food. They patted the baby's head, clutched the soft thigh and watched as she kicked and wiggled.

The two older boys stood on the opposite side from the three seated guardians. They stepped from foot to foot with a restless movement that continued even as they ate. The boys sent out arrowlike glances that soared above and beyond the elder's heads to hook onto the roof of the small building at the top of the hill. They recapped their dives. Then the dart of hunger struck again to be quickly but brutally answered by their own swinging arm and hand that brought the ham sandwich into mouth followed by a gulp of orange soda, a flurry of bubbles—a corrosive stream of liquid that carried down the quickly chewed food.

Ellen, Kate, and Bill, enthroned below, understood that the boys were behaving normally. In line with the boy's flight path, they were hit with fallen debris from the in-flight crash. It hit them on the head or on the arm, nicked their cheeks, and occasionally landed in their laps. They could laugh; it was part of that familiar geographical, physiological and psychological map pinned to the wall of their semiprivate domain of thought.

Lunch broke up.

The children chased one another in the shallow water. They pushed the water with their palms and their raised knees as if trying to form something out of the otherwise large flat puddle. One of the larger boys ignored a littler one's demands to return her plastic fishing rod. The younger one tugged and whined while the other vigorously tested the toy's functionality. Bill arrived to mediate the conflict. He soon returned to his seat positioned between the two older women. The three of them formed a gentle arc at the crest of the grassy slope that led down to the wading pool. Bill settled in and the back and forth, listen and be heard, well-woven conversation resumed.

Mary gathered the empty soda cans and stacked the soiled paper plates, stuffing them into a large garbage bag.

"The problem with Jesse is that he refuses to hear any criticism whatsoever." Mary spoke vaguely in the right direction, but neither Bill nor the other two women responded to her observation.

Little Lucy ran up to the elders with a small bundle of daisies and yanked grass held tightly in her chubby hand. She pressed herself between one woman's knees, her round belly seeking to be held.

"Ellen, make me a crown. I want a crown. Ellen, make me a crown now."

Ellen twisted the grass and flowers into a flimsy braid to fold into the little girl's hair.

"There you go, darling. Now you look like a princess. Go and show Suri."

With a flat pat she tapped the girl's shoulder.

Mary pulled the two handles of the plastic bag into a knot. "Lucy, didn't I tell you to get your shoes on? You are not going in that water until you put them on."

"Mary, none of the other children are—I really don't think there is a problem here."

"That's your opinion, but I have a right to say what I think is best for her. She's my niece and I'm responsible for her. No matter what, I don't want Lucy to go in without her plastic sandals. There could be glass or a sharp stone. The last thing I want is a trip to the emergency room."

"Listen Mary—I'll tell you what—if Lucy steps on a piece of glass, I will take her to the emergency room—Really Mary, I think it is all right."

"Hah! That's very comforting. After this, guess who Lucy is going to listen to. I'm only trying to do what is best for her and all of you get in my way. Fine. It's too late now." Mary tried to take Lucy by the hand but the little girl turned the hand into a fist and struck the big woman on the thigh before running breathlessly to the water.

"It's all right Mary, take it easy. Children forget everything. Why don't you take a walk and buy the kids some ice cream?"

"I'm feeling tired. I'm going over there to lie down." Mary walked toward the lake and spread out her towel and lay still and inert with eyes closed.

Kate turned to Rachel, the young mother, with baby Louisa cradled in her arms, "You know, Rachel, Mary is crippled in a way you and I will never be."

Kate paused and with an affected sadness and careful emphasis continued, "she is an emotional cripple."

"You can say that again!"

"I really get so angry with her sometimes and have to remind myself of that. First of all, she is not very intelligent. She is a big, awkward woman and so aggressive!

"Emotionally speaking she has the maturity of a 12-year-old—if that. You know, her childhood must have been a nightmare: poverty, abuse—the whole works. Who knows what Mary has had to endure—I hate to think about it! Now she's with us—she's gotta live with somebody, right? I just have to know how to cool myself down. It's hard to live with her. And especially hard in a situation like this when everyone just wants to relax and enjoy one another. She really doesn't have a clue about how to relate to us. She's an angry, wounded woman who will probably never change. It's sad, but that's the way it is."

Rachel steered her slightly swollen nipple into the baby's groping mouth and drew down on her breast to ease the flow of milk. Kate looked on with a serious but appreciative gaze before somberly raising her head to scan the grounds. She identified the position of each member of the clan and reported the activity of each to the present company.

Baby Louisa sucked rhythmically occasionally letting her eyelids flutter closed. She brought her little hand close to her mouth and scratched at her mothers white breast. "It drives me crazy when she tells me how to take care of Louisa. She's never even been a

50

mother! And she does it in such a pushy way. Last night she said: 'don't spoil the baby' . . . she told me to leave Louisa crying in her crib and that I hold her too much. I knew Louisa had gas—that's why she was screaming! She really doesn't know what she is talking about, but she still sticks her nose into other people's business.

"I won't let her pick up my baby . . . Actually last night David and I were talking about Mary. He thinks she is not a good influence on the kids. She's too negative. He said maybe she should just stick to the custodial work."

David was playing catch with the older boys and little Lucy. The upper half of him caught and threw the ball while his lower half was tugged at and pulled by the thickset little girl. Lucy screamed with delight at being thrown hither and thither by his body movements.

Grass, asphalt, grass and Mary's body lying prone on the bit of sloped ground across from the lake. I kept an eye on her as I approached the lake's edge. Mary up close. I saw the yellowed undersoles of her feet, the thick-knuckled toes. I followed her unshaven legs into the khaki shorts snapped over a floral patterned bathing suit. I paused at her sturdy breasts bolstered by the bathing suit's wire frame and padded inlay.

I care about Mary—and her body thickened by its built-in armor. The armor encases her torso. The torso houses her organs. Fatty tissue surrounds every eccentric sac and the molded functional muscles that are held in the hull of that torso. There is another type of fatty tissue that is unattached; it floats in between ridiculing the organ's stress and strain—their lack of freedom, their exhaustion; these miniature clouds of fat that brush against the hardening cords and ruffled edges of her yellowed ligaments are both obstructive and inspiringly free.

I care about Mary's thick muscular arms: their clear functionality. This attribute of unquestionable functionality impresses me as something beautiful. The arms don't belong to Mary. They belong to the tasks she performs: sweeping, tucking, picking up, lifting, and carrying, carrying, carrying.

I dove into the lake's cool water. I swam out and back and several times around. As I was pulling myself out of the water I saw Mary had now risen from her bed. She looked like a giant beside the little girl.

Taking hold of her hand, Suri pulled Mary toward the lake, singing a name: Mary, Mary, Maaary. The ground ended abruptly with a sharp drop to the water below. As she threw her wiry but supple body into the water, each one of her evenly browned and slender limbs caught a ray of sunlight. Her child's arms reached out of the water: powerful and lean of excess. Even in the area of the lake where she could still touch bottom, Suri walked on the tips of her toes. She flapped her arms and splashed. From the depth of her taut little belly she called: "Mary, come on, Mary—jump—just jump. Mary! Come on—jump!" Mary dropped her heavy self onto the ladder's first step and then the second: pflunk, pflunk. With a wincing but winking face, she reached timidly out to the water and finally let her body slip off the ladder. A bit of water splashed in her face and up her nose, forcing her to cough. Catching up with a greater feeling of buoyancy, Mary made a steady effort to reach the little girl. She took large ostrichlike steps. She stretched her arms out across the water and drew them back in an arc mimicking the breast stroke as she made her way.

She breathed in and out slowly in time with her steps, lowering her face toward the surface without actually touching it. It was a coherent simulation. Mary arrived and little Suri, all spokes around a wheel, assaulted her. She spun around Mary's solid body. She demanded Mary lift her kicking body into the air and then toss it away: splash. Suri wrapped her arms around Mary's neck. Mary swished the little girl's body through the water: back and forth, side to side, or up and down. Her hold unclasped. For whatever reasons. And Suri squirmed away toward the platform. She spun alone, treading water, drunk on the wide expanse of the lake, drunk on the rich, shadowy green of the trees, drunk on the feeling of water all around her. All her energy spent in a wanton drunkeness, Suri again wanted Mary to hold her. She cried out, "Mary!" drawing out the open vowel—baahing like a lamb—believing that her voice had the power to pull the big woman toward her.

I watched Mary take a few strokes: she swam—until something deserted her. She was no longer swimming; her buoyancy gave way to gravity and she started to sink.

The clever, athletic child didn't understand what was happening; was this a game? Stop Mary! Mary tried to bring herself above water. She made gurgling sounds, speech mixed with water, words and sounds rising bubblelike, trying to burst into the air, were swallowed up by the water again. What was bringing Mary down? Suri started to scream. Ellen hears first. Oh my God! She turns to Kate. Rachel hears. Rachel's arms are full with the baby. Rachel stays seated and looks at Louisa, her living anchor; she cannot leave the baby alone. David runs over. He looks over first to Suri—then to Mary's flailing arms. He is completely dressed. Should he jump directly in the water or first peel off his clothes? The elders have raised themselves from the lawn chairs—and are jogging as fast as they can to the lakes edge. As they raise leg after leg, their heads hang low, surprisingly heavy. David has taken off his pants and dives into the water. He understands now; he might be too late now. The elders understand. They are as helpless as before. Mary has disappeared. David dives to retrieve her and pulls her big, dripping body up. She breaks out of the water: big and colorful. The sky once again touches her head. He swims her to the lake edge. She is so heavy. He is strong. He is making a great effort but maybe it's too late. Suri is still standing on the platform; she is screaming in rhythmic yelps: she is a lovable dog: wet and loyal. She is an unstoppable alarm and there is now a small crowd at the edge of the lake. Mary is sprawled on the grass encircled by everyone. David's mouth is over her gaping mouth. He pinches her nostrils shut. Breathing and counting. Bill is there. He is on his knees beside Mary. As soon as he gets the signal, Bill thumps her on the chest. One, two, three—pause. Again. One, two, three. Rachel strokes the baby's head. She is communicating something desperately to the baby's head. Scratching, digging, trying to grab back what she had only moments earlier thought was so worthless. Big old Mary, sprawled on the grass: looking so waxy, bluish around the eyes. Mary's dead. Steve hears the whisper in his head. He feels something ticklish in his chest and in his ear at the same time. Ha, ha, ha, psss, dead. Suri is squawking. She has turned into a goose or a gull. Her arms are flapping up and down: those beautiful lithe brown arms. Everyone else is close by now, even Mary. Only Suri is far away: it's as if she were behind bars, in the zoo. Who called the ambulance? Here they are. In their white coats and white pants. The path through the crowd, the stretcher; the path back to the ambulance parked on the grass. There are tracks in the grass all the way to the road. The white van with frosted back windows drives away. Large tracts of lawn are ruined. The many people that have gathered around the accident start to walk back to where they were before.

Jesse swims to Suri. He climbs up to the platform and brings her trembling body close to his. He squeezes her so tightly that he feels that he is squeezing himself. A man with a big red face, wearing a uniform sidles up to the platform. He directs the children into the rowboat and throws a large blanket over each. He rows the two children to the shore.

The circle broke apart: dispersal. Mary's family returned to where they had been sitting a short while before.

I would never know with my own arms how heavy she really was.

David was faster. They passed me, the swimmer and the body—going the opposite direction back toward the shore. It was once again a big lake—rarely crowded.

I often ask myself why my trigger was delayed. Had I thought I hadn't the strength? Had I simply been watching this woman for such a while that I failed to grasp that I could do something other than observe her? Or was I frightened by the prospect of being so intimately connected to this woman's tenuous connection to the living.

Give it a chance, I told myself, another perspective on these events might emerge. Needless to say, when my husband and children returned, I hugged them dearly. I was very motherly for several weeks following.

Escape

"I'm going to escape," she said turning toward me and away from me at one and the same time. Escape from a needy, clinging child and from habit. Escape a daily repeating series of mirror-studded panoramas assembled to achieve a semblance of purpose. Escape from scenes that have the irresistible capacity to disengage her from her own fleeing and flowing desire. She can still laugh with despair! But this morning the overriding idea was to arrive somewhere else willfully.

I watched her as she placed both hands on her small daughter's shoulders as if to establish an undeniable concern and unalterable connection and the possibility that an arm's length distance can stretch—stretch into an infinity—at least for a time, at least long and far enough to give birth to the knowledge that a mother and her child do not and will never again occupy the same ground.

The new idea that determined position might alter everything slipped into action.

Her larger hands and sparse but reassuring words supplying an effective and quick summary of the situation: Find your seat over there, darling, the class is about to begin. These directions transformed into a pointing limb attached to a torso and to another pair of restless already departing limbs, unable not to use the floor, and this last cue as the marker for the beginning of the race against time: to escape, to arrive and to return in time.

When she reached the street, it was clear that her escape to somewhere else would be successful. It was exactly at this moment, when she allowed herself the slightest pause to recognize the accomplishment, that her right foot tripped on her left. The two feet were not yet similarly informed of her purpose: the right foot perhaps believing that something had already been forgotten.

I Was Sitting Alone

I was sitting alone in the late afternoon, reading, concentrating on receiving what it was I felt offered, there on the page, when he started talking to me. He cajoled, coaxed, teased and provoked, insisting with his two round, glistening eyes that I listen to what he had to say.

As always my ears were open; I believe my ears are always open even when other people tell me they are not. It could be possible that I forget those moments when I am not paying attention to anything beside the rumblings of an impending storm. Then I am only listening to the instinctive shutting of windows and retracing the recovered sequence of linked corridors used in emergencies.

He said, "You think you can get away like that? It's that easy, isn't it, to slip out and slide away." And he lengthened the "I" in slide so I would feel my own deceptive character as he experienced it and as he believed it to be.

But I was reading, sitting alone in the late afternoon, and wanting it that way: wanting to receive what I imagined the words on the page offered. I told him then that I didn't want to listen—that I didn't want him there at all. That I wished he would turn away and stop staring, that I didn't want to be stared at in that way and that I wanted him to go.

I told him he had to leave, that his eyes should recede, back away from their aggressive performance, that I didn't want them staring at me inquiringly.

Monopoly

Javier was lying in bed next to Sabrina telling her why he wouldn't be going to work at Papa's anymore. He told her it was going to be a long story, so she let that pretty little head she'd been propping up cupped in her hand drop into the pillow. Javier was looking up at the ceiling and so was she. Then he started talking, glad to be watching it all again with her lying there next to him.

We were playing Monopoly and big fat Mama Maria was shaking the dice in her hand. I don't know how she did it but she could make the dice click louder than any of us. The thin guy with the chisel marks still in his face steps out from behind the bar and pulls up a chair next to Mama. The dice roll out, and it is a two and a four. Mama moves her thimble over to Park Place, just as if she knew that was where she would be going—no matter what. Of course she had plenty of money to buy it. She gets the card and sits back in her chair. Meanwhile, the bartender has wrapped his arm around her, just below the shoulder, and he's lucky his arm is long enough, because the next thing you know he's petting her big boobs like they were for everybody to share: house pets or something. She didn't seem to mind; she was smiling, lolling her head side to side as if there were music playing and clicking her tongue. Her eyes were really twinkling. Of course she was winning—like always we were trailing behind, either waiting in the poorhouse, or in jail, but still eager to play. Then the door with the decorative glass inlay rattled, which meant Papa Borracho had come home. Chiselface gets up and slips back behind the bar. He starts vigorously sudsing glasses, pumping them one by one on the brush. I knew Mama wanted to keep on playing but she folds up the board anyway, knocking the pieces into the box. The pale green cards got all mixed up with the pale yellow ones, and the board wasn't settling down well enough to close the box evenly. I ran and slipped it onto the shelf in the employee coat closet and ran back to the table to clear away the glasses. We all took our places and put on bored faces.

"It looks really bad in here," he said. "Yeah, I think it stinks. Who's been farting? I'm not surprised there are no customers in a stinking place like this." My belly started to cramp and I was about to go to the back and get my coat and get the fuck out before something awful happened. I was in no mood for a bad scene and it was crystal clear that one was on its way.

Then he shouts, "Who the fuck's got a light!" Papa's strutting around pushing anybody in his way, still shouting, "Which one of you got a light!" No one wanted to go near him. Finally Chiselface walked over, step, step, step in his dancer's shoes, and lit Papa's baby cigar. I couldn't lift my face from the floorboards and I noticed that I was holding my breath in order to make as little sound as possible when I breathed. Luckily, Mama Maria sauntered over to Papa, just about bumping into him with her big breasts and says, "Let's close up early tonight, baby, and go out to eat. I've been cooped up here all day. I can't stand the stink either . . . I'm sick of all their faces—Let's close up and go out, hmm?"

We could all tell he was thinking it over. He was trying not to admit to himself that nobody was interested in having a plate of over-cooked *pollo con arroz* with a glass of piss-flavored beer in this hole in the wall. So he was taking his time to think of a different way to interpret the situation. The moment Papa Borracho would say yes, it would be as though a hundred fireflies were let loose—their tail-lights blinking and their heads banging into chairs, doors and walls. Knowing that we wouldn't be spending the evening being hit by the spit-coated insults that flew out of Papa's mouth would make our tight little asses start twitching.

Even though it was possible Papa would say, "Yeah, O.K." and this hunk of bad tasting pork might even waddle out of here, I knew he wanted to hurt somebody first. He had that need to stick his stinger in somebody's face just to hear them cry. He liked to hurt. And Mama, she liked getting in between. She was built for that. It was beyond me to imagine how many stingers her warm body had intercepted or if they had left any scars.

"Yes—No—Yes—No," we were all watching the bouncing ball. Those of us who were still sitting, like me, for example, could feel the tickle caused by the sweating in the seat of the pants. Papa didn't say anything—

perhaps he was just too dumb to decide. In my opinion, he still wanted to do something bad. He was bursting with badness—he oozed with it.

But when he pushed Mama to the side, that surprised me. He lay the seat of his hand on that spot where the two halves of the ribcage meet and where the stomach is hiding, which for Mama lies deep behind lots of skin and flesh. There must be more of Mama Maria there than in anywhere else in her body.

Papa swung around looking for a target. She was new. She wasn't pretty. And it was clear she'd soon be gone. So Papa walks up and takes her chin in his hand.

"Lipstick. Every girl here wears lipstick. But you don't think you need to, do you Miss Ugly. But you're wrong, totally wrong." Then Papa lifts the poor girls skirt and with his shoe pulls down her sock—cause that's what she was wearing. He drags his finger along her shin and says, "How do you like that, she's a real bearded lady. Now I really like that, don't you boys?"

Then he says so sweetly, "Darling, next time you come to serve in my restaurant, try hiding your ugly face a bit better. I like to see pretty girls—ladies all made up and—please, shave off the fur—or don't bring your butch face back here again."

So what does this bookworm of a girl do? She bends down and pulls up her wooly sock slowly and carefully so it rests in exactly the right place just below the knee. Then she slips her own hand under her skirt and pulls down her little panty. She squats right there in the middle of the restaurant and makes a little puddle—actually it's a good-sized pool! She straightens up, looking very satisfied and wiggles back into her bitty slip. She reaches behind her back and unties her apron. She shakes it out right on top. The coins, the bills—a few crumpled pieces slide like paper boats on the water. Then she folds the apron into a neat little packet and hands it to good Old Papa, whose cigar is dangling dangerously over his bristly-edged lower lip.

The best part is that he actually sticks out his chubby paw to receive it. The girl then walks over to the employee closet, gets her coat and walks out. First we are looking at Papa—what the hell is he going to do now, we're thinking. Another guy has to step out of the way to avoid being touched by the piss spreading in fat lines across the floor. I can't look away from the wet money and I'm almost smiling making a picture of the poor fool who is going eventually to fish it all out. The rest are just staring at the door long after it makes its last rattle. Then one by one and in twos until there is almost a crowd around the closet, we all get our coats and leave. (Of course no one else shakes out his or her apron—God knows we all need the money!)

Child

A woman is putting her child to sleep. The room is dark. The child will not settle down. Despite the woman's reassuring words, the child gropes for the mother's body with a fearful whimpering.

Along the road a motorcycle issues a loud purr. It's late and for a moment the woman is angered by the rider's thoughtlessness. Silently, the mother protests: such a sound will disturb so many children just drifting off to sleep.

Stretching out beside the child, the mother imagines just what the biker feels. Immediately she understands that tonight she would accept his offer. Black velvet air, wind, turns and straight aways and then taut skin. So many phantom sensations percolate.

Lifting the child's limp sleeping arm off her leg, she is surprised that she feels more immediate compassion for the man than she does for her own child.

Suburban Rodeo

Suburban Rodeo is a franchise operation. Versions exist in Tokyo and most major cities in Japan. One was also recently built beside the Ch'yongdok Palace and the Olympic Hilton in Seoul. Its developers distributed a promotional pilot targeting chronic insomniacs. Following a successful series of late-night airings, P.F.B. Rodeos® (prefabricated rings) were installed just about everywhere. Rodeos take place nightly during the compromised hours when most people sleep. Anybody has a chance to play a role in a Suburban Rodeo. You are given a choice from the line-up of late-night cowboys, master of ceremonies, one of ten pretty bar girls, a stable boy, and the guy in gray overalls who rakes smooth the sand in the arena between performances.

Many women enter the monthly R.Q.C., Rodeo Queen Contest.

Financed with loans from the Japanese subsidiary of General Mills and the Korean chewing gum giant, Lotte, most Suburban Rodeos feature a gift shop where the new line of colorful Styrofoam cups used throughout the complex can be purchased in festive 12-packs.

In F.S.N.Y. (Fresh Style New York), the Suburban Rodeo fills the center of the sport track. The passage to the arena, inserted between two over-the-counter snack bars, is a horseshoe-shaped doorway cut out of illuminated acrylic panels and bordered with over one hundred miniature stage lights.

First of all, a dream can recur. Upon waking, it is not that easy for you to distinguish the slight variations.

A Suburban Rodeo can excite recurrent dreams. Squashed by the typical futility of each workday, the insomniac rehatches himself as a night predator prepared to dominate the small hours of the night. The world is in effect smaller then and offers the insomniac unlimited chances to exercise his unchecked power to track down and mount the pretty pink-skinned inflated girls known as pink elephants.

The Suburban Rodeo is a nightly story of losers dressed as cowboys slipping out of place in the round up. Contrary to expectation, there are no prizewinners. There are only profiteers.

Titles and schedules are distributed to the cowboys when they pass the secretary's desk on their way to the dressing rooms. She and her two assistants plan this evening's roll call.

The question of costume is not left to chance. The evening show is envisioned through the clothes the players wear.

The woman behind the desk— she is the stage manager— asks each his size. Every man falls into one of five categories. There are quotas for each. Five sizes, five dressing rooms, and seven to ten contestants for each nightly show. The fatter ones flirt with her, trying to distract her from her careful accounting.

One hour is given to dress, make-up, and general instruction. The master of ceremonies gives a formal introduction. The technical advisor outlines advisable precautions and safety measures. "You are all amateurs," he says, "don't forget that."

During the preparations, tonight's cowboys are both silent and somber or display a reckless confidence. In the last ten minutes prior to the start of the show, they study one another carefully and without shyness. Of course each wants to know some telling detail about his fellow competitors.

Before the show begins, they are kept waiting in a small auxiliary room beside the ring.

At least three of the men leaf through the magazines arranged on the two small coffee tables. The room is a little too warm. Two of the men stand up and perform preparatory exercises. They touch their toes and do no less than ten knee bends accompanied by an even number of deeply drawn breaths. After finishing, one remains standing while the other seeks out the men's room down the hall.

Minutes later, a small plain woman enters the room and reads from her clipboard the name of the first contestant.

He stands up and is led out of the room and down another long corridor divided by a boldly painted wainscoting.

The remaining cowboys concentrate on wearing serious expressions. An older one of the group gets up and switches on the TV monitor that is positioned in one corner of the room.

The first contestant has already been hoisted into position. Where is the horse? There have been no introductions.

Something about what is waiting below the cowboy's legs spread and poised in a herringbone configuration is wild and unpredictable. Is this why the cowboy is here? No, the cowboy is here to win, to play a key role in tonight's program.

With squinting eyes, the cowboy looks out at the sandy-colored floor of the arena and then into the spectators' flattened faces. The audience has been drinking beer from colored Styrofoam cups. Most of them are smiling.

The cowboy contestant feels exposed. Where is his hat? A big brimmed white cowboy hat came with his outfit. He can't remember where he set it down. Wasn't it in his hands when the lady first entered the room? And hadn't he put it on his head as they walked down the corridor together? Had he dropped it on the ground when they lifted him into place, or had he handed it . . .

And then everything happened so fast—the deafening bell, the blood rushing to his head, his heart pumping hard and that sudden drop—onto the wild thing below.

Together they were thrown into the ring.

The horse pulled him into the arena, his wildness arching elegantly and as if in spasm.

Mechanically, the horse exercised itself. The cowboy gave way to the cresting waves and let his legs swing upward in time with the animal's jolts.

But the cowboy makes a false move. He misunderstands the beast's program.

The wildness toys violently with his miscomprehension. He throws the limp cowboy up and off. The fall is not without impact. The audience screams and screeches with delight.

Two employees dressed in white lab coats carry out the fallen cowboy. They act like hospital interns in charge of a nonambulant patient. The first contestant is returned to the correct dressing room. He undresses and replaces the clothes to the appropriate hanger. With hurried movements he slips into his own clothes. The pretty stage manager is waiting beside the dressing room door. A voice sputters through the intercom hitting the corridor walls. She brings him to a rear exit.

He had bad luck. He should not have been the first to go. The fallen cowboy looked back at the building and the small door marked emergency exit. He was not a prizewinner. That much was clear.

At the first corner, he waits for a taxi. He checks his watch. There is little traffic and he must therefore wait a while before any empty taxis appear. His body is exhausted. He finds it soothing to stare down the road and see the line of stars produced by the road lights. Even when standing, he dozes intermittently. Later, in the taxi the voice of the radio announcer is interrupted by the cowboy's heavy snores.

Baby Beckett

The foaming, growling mouth snagged on a thorn bites the bit at its stem. The mouth bites its way through complication. So too did Beckett, the baby, gnaw at his mother's supple breast, his still little mouth invaded by teeth. Selflessly she continued to nurse him, and to muffle her cries, despite the pain and shallow wounding.

Against her soundly bedded wish, the milk no longer flowed freely. The bounty over, her nipples hung low with her breasts somewhat smaller than before.

Little Samuel was not robust. He could not be. Nor did he cry for more.

He sat still: a day, a day, a day, economic in all his ways.

His worried mother would thrash about like a trapped bird and then swoop down, scoop him up and peck at him with hard little kisses. Later she would scream and screech, issuing a string of unintelligible sounds at once experimental and out of control.

Horizontal Drainage

Jannis invents her mother and her mother's mother. The two older women stem from her younger body and feed off her urgent inquiry. Jannis cannot believe that her mother and the ghost of her mother's mother had never asked the important questions. Jannis' mother has never corrected her daughter's oversight.

Jannis' mother also invents. Her inventions appear simultaneously with the cartographic contours she draws around herself and which she has retraced for over 50 years.

Succeeding map by model, model by map in turn: this is the first complicity between mother and daughter.

Jannis and her mother can both agree that Jannis' grandmother has never existed as a fully realized invention. She appears as gesture, dried-up, with no blood and no bones. Jannis' grandmother functions like a metronome ticking out a suggestive time.

Jannis' grandmother was in the kitchen preparing a Kassler Braten for the Thursday evening meal. The Kassler lay like part of a hollowed-out log on the kitchen table. Kneeling, with chest pressed against the back of the sofa, Jannis' mother perched her head on the cushioned rim in order to get a comfortable view out the living room window. From her station by the window, she waited for each hard knock as one after another cutlet shaped piece of meat was sheared off the log by the sure swing of her mother's cleaver.

The living room walls were painted in deep dark red panels framed in shiny white moldings; floral rings barely emerged from the high ceiling. The Oriental carpets, etched glass, polished wood frames of precious and decorative woods were of exemplary craftsmanship and quality.

The couch had its soft parts and its hard parts. A smooth wood sphere completed the well-padded man-sized armrest. The leather upholstered armchairs, the oval tea table, the yellow ochre lampshade with fringe border . . .

Jannis demands that her mother remember more. *What is happening beyond the window? How much can you see—are they shouting? Do the Jews enter the trains without protest? Can't you hear screams? I can't imagine the people not putting up protest. Some of them must be your neighbors. Don't you recognize anyone? Mama! How do you feel, watching all this?*

The living room was warm. The windows had not been opened since the Sunday before. Jannis' mother felt sleepy. She was on holiday. School would not begin until Monday and she had no special meetings planned. She had been sitting in the living room since the end of breakfast. Gazing all morning out the window had left Jannis' mother tired and a bit dull-witted. She couldn't be sure if she had heard shouting outside. If she had, it was certainly muffled. Jannis' grandmother was cooking the Kassler Braten for the midday meal. The smell had begun to reach the living room. In a few hours the guests would arrive. Jannis' grandmother was known for her Kassler Braten.

Jannis' family lives in her mother's childhood house. In fact, Jannis' mother has never lived anywhere else.

Outside were coats, so many coats. Coats clustered shoulder to shoulder. The dark ones outnumbered the colored. A few red coats and even white ones could be picked out—children usually wore those.

The police pushed them along. Many eyes were looking for something to fix on. Jannis' mother watched this from her window. They were being deported . . . but at the time she didn't see it in that way.

No, I don't remember recognizing anyone.

The train had been parked all morning. It stood at least 100 meters away from the station proper. Jannis' mother had noticed it standing there when she opened the front door to bring in the three bottles of fresh milk before breakfast.

From the living room window she could keep two entire cars and a half of a third in view without getting up from her position on the couch. A row of soot-blackened windows ran along the top of each wagon. Or perhaps they were simply painted over with dark paint. From such a distance it was difficult to distinguish.

No, let me remember—they were not windows at all. A narrow row of vents with slats turned to the horizontal position ran along the top of each wagon. She could not make out this detail clearly enough to say how it was. She counted one, two, three . . . five openings. Beside a slightly open door she could just make out a hand disappearing into the shadows. Jannis' mother traced along the hand's profile. The concentration strained her eye muscles but there was something satisfying in her ability to feel closer, to fight the corrosive power of the shadows and the distance between herself and the hand. She clings to this detail.

The sudden gunshot threw her back on her bottom. Then there was the galloping rhythm of the slats slapping shut. When she returned to her station the openings were closed and the thick shadows gone.

Jannis' grandmother called out through the open kitchen door. She asks Jannis' mother to buy a bottle of *Weizenkorn Schnapps* for the guests to enjoy after the midday meal. Of course Jannis' grandmother is too busy with the preparations to go herself. Be a dear, child, and run down to Stolz's liquor shop. Buy a bottle of *Schnapps*. Mr. Stolz knows which one we like. There is money in my purse, by the door. Go ahead, take it yourself, my hands are not clean.

Jannis' mother slipped into her father's great coat that always hung in the closet by the front door. She stuffed a ten mark bill she had found in her mother's purse into the miniature handkerchief pocket. She reconsidered and removed the bill to one of two breast pockets hidden in the inner lining.

To reach the shopping street Jannis' mother was accustomed to walk alongside the tracks for about 500 meters. As it was a day in early March the air was still fresh and cool. She walked with her eyes partially closed and leisurely reviewed the image of the train car returning to mind. Being outside made it easier for her to understand the relative size of things.

From her house, the land sloped down toward the tracks. The train's adjoining cars must have been hidden by the patch of linden trees that in recent years had grown so thick and tall. Satisfied with her own reasoning, she opened her eyes more fully. She had already reached the first block of stores and offices belonging to her neighborhood.

The sun at her back was low enough to give her a long and thin shadow to follow. She laughed at how her father's coat distinguished her slightly unfamiliar silhouette. In the middle of the first block she was nearing Stein's Liquor Store. As she had been walking very close to the wall of buildings to catch a good look at herself in the display windows, the bold strokes of white paint making up the word

'*JUDE*' jumped right out at her. She pressed her cheek up to the glass and looked in.

The place was a complete wreck. The wood shelves once integrated into the walls had been pulled down to the floor. Disorderly stacks and piles of paper were strewn randomly across the floor along with sharp fragments of wood broken off from the shelves. A row of naked bulbs described an obscene axis down the middle of the ceiling. The carefully etched glass spheres that once covered of them were all simply gone. There was only one bottle of alcohol visible in the entire store. Embraced by the soft cast shadow of the letter 'U', it stood open on the dusty step of the display window at the front of the store. A rod of light passed through the glass animating the small amount of clear amber spirits still remaining in the bottle.

Searching the large shadows in the store tired her. Jannis' mother returned to her feet and remembering her charge continued on to Mr. Stolz' shop which was at the first corner of the next block.

Mr. Stolz climbed up a few steps on the ladder attached to a track on the upper edge of the shelves at Jannis' mother's request for the bottle of *Weizenkorn Schnapps*. Here, my dear, he said and handed the bottle to her wrapped in white paper twisted into place at the bottle's neck. Jannis' mother thanked him, nodded to his assistant and left the store with her purchase. Once outside she slipped the bottle into the spacious front pocket of her father's great coat and started walking back in the same way she came. Although Mr. Stolz and his employee had not made any signs to acknowledge that Jannis' mother was wearing a man's coat, once outside, she began a count of the number of people who stole a second glance at her figure as she passed by. The majority of those to examine her most closely were women of all ages, both young and old.

Jannis' mother cut diagonally across a small park to a narrow dirt path that ran closer alongside the tracks than the paved road.

The train was now less than thirty meters to her left. Jannis' mother recognized one of the cars as that she had been so closely examining from the living room window. There was its identification number and the swatch of black paint almost in the middle of the car. Her fascination in comparing the two viewpoints drew her closer to the train.

She was studying the rust pattern below the window when she felt someone grip her arm hard. She whipped around and was relieved to see the face of a policeman. His face also looked familiar. She smiled pleasantly and explained that she was on her way home from the liquor shop where she had made a purchase for her mother. The policeman did not return her smile. He pushed Jannis' mother toward the train. She fell against a family of four huddled in a group in front of the steps to the car door. The man in uniform yelled at these people to enter the train and motioned with a nod of the head that Jannis' mother should do the same. Pointing to the rather large house behind the poplars she told him again that it was her house. She said she must go home, but the policeman ignored her pleas. He pushed her roughly up the stairs and through the door. On the second step, she slipped on the long skirts of her father's great coat.

The sight within the car made her gasp. All of the seats had been ripped out of the car. Everybody was standing. The car was so packed with bodies that no one had even enough room to remove his coat. The heavy air stank of sweat and wool coats worn all winter without wash. She gulped the air as if she were choking.

She protested. You have made a mistake. I am not Jewish. I live here, in that house, there. It was no longer visible from within the train. She spoke surrounded only by the Jews. She yelled out her protest even more loudly but to no avail. She was a rock sinking in the big sea.

The policeman was the only figure who could cut a path across the car. He had a stick in his hand. No one tried to smother him or to deny him a free way. He enjoyed a steady stream of oxygen rich air. He seemed certain to survive. He was employed, and he performed his job effectively. And he would do so too, tomorrow and the day after.

She realized now it was the coat she wore. What rightfully minded person would wear an absurdly oversized coat in public? Unless it was already clear that, permanently dwarfed and thwarted, one was already an outsider.

She could envision her pirouette to freedom that let it be known who she was. When freed her arms and legs would succeed to pull the rest of her self above it all. She was absolutely certain that she was not and could never be Jewish.

Jannis' mother began to twist in place. She shows her daughter how she was able to distinguish herself from the wool fold that wove so many into one suffering body.

With eyes closed she pressed her body against the others, turning in place to release the loosely held buttons. With one flap free, she twisted further trying to catch the open flap of her coat between her body and theirs. She believed in this possibility that the coat could fall away. Let them tug it off her pretty shoulders. She was a German girl in the midst of a pubescent bloom. She often counted the six new firm buds on her body.

The coat fell to her feet.

If she was mistaken for a Jew, it was clearly because she was wearing a wool coat several sizes too big. Janis' mother made the vague assumption that a Jew might do such a thing. For example, the family is too poor to buy every member of the family a winter coat, so the eldest girl must wear the coat of her recently deceased grandfather. Perhaps a Jewish girl had been stupid enough to convince herself that she could conceal her identity by wearing a grossly oversized coat and thereby sneak away unattended.

But Jannis' mother had a vision of herself. Her bare arms and shoulders emerged from a well-tailored tunic dress. The dress was sewn from an eye-catching light red cloth. Her legs were also bare. (She wore leather thong sandals.) Her hair was carefully brushed away from a freshly washed face.

She climbed onto the shoulders of one of them. He was a middle-aged father of two. His wife in her plain kerchief helped her up. The wife was in fact very kind and had no objections when Jannis' mother sat up on the shoulders of her husband of 15 years. Jannis' mother sat there, supple and confident and remembered the many times she had sat, with back straight on the back of her cousin's pony.

But the ceiling of the train was too low for her to sit up. She shifted into a different position, stretching out between two sets of shoulders as if the move were part of a gymnastic routine. She knew she had a fine voice. She would break into song. The melody would be simple, a song everybody should know.

Jannis' mother's eyes were shut tight. They opened of themselves with the policeman's staccato orders that each passenger must produce personal identification for inspection.

Jannis' mother was allowed to return home—*Does someone recognize you? Does someone recognize your name? What is it that makes the guard believe your story?*

She would never know. He looked at her. He took her chin in his hand. He examined her shoes and the buttons of her blouse and its sleeves. At the end he nodded to another man standing nearby who escorted Jannis' mother off the train. They all followed her with their eyes until she breathed the fresh air again.

She blew through the door to her parents' house as the food was being brought to the table. She did not attempt to report what had happened to her. She had not yet understood herself. In response to her mother's inquiry, she ran back to the foyer and pulled out the white wrapped bottle from the pocket of the borrowed coat.

Her mother fell silent. The story seemed to have come to an end. They remained seated across from one another at the now already cleared dining room table. Jannis' mother's hands busied themselves in forming a tiny pile of crumbs with the fallen bits of the home-made apple cake shared by mother and daughter for the afternoon tea. Jannis sat still and rigid. She exerted herself by staring at her mother's figure. With her gaze locked in place she examined the puffy face and wavy blond hair. Every millimeter came under magnified scrutiny. She was intent to reduce her mother to her most elemental composition in order to declare as impossible her own physical similarity to this woman. She could no longer look on this woman as her mother and rejected this possibility outright as an impossible mistake.

Jannis made no response when her mother addressed her by name. Eventually she left the room. Jannis remained seated, watching nothing. Dusk fell. She slid off her seat and out of the room when she heard her father's heavy footsteps approach. The rest of the evening she lay on her bed vaguely listening to the muffled voices rising from below. They were speaking about her but she was too numb to be stirred. When she was sure everyone was asleep she sat up and left the house. She caught the last train to Friedrichstraße.

An Open Mouth

This is in memory of a particular execution. Someone's slipping down the stairs: racing down the stairs—No! They threw her down: guns pinned to their hands, barrel sliding out of its skin-lined pocket, guns poking through the gap between the ears, as if to execute hearing. It's rumored that she meant to be a heroine.

An open mouth. Open in submission to being clubbed, clogged or brutally disfigured. Open for the sake of being open: to receive the coming blow. Open to die open: a hole in the closure inflicted from outside. Baring its teeth: a show of tight lipped muscularity: the ability to hold the hole—opening for breath incoming and outgoing—opening for screams forcing their way out irregardless of the position of mouth or of body—the mouth is held open.

Then, regaining its usual instrumentality, lips slack or pursed, interacting with teeth, or the last puffs of air pressed flat, the hole fades: becomes immaterial.

Earthworms

The executioner orders his victims to stand in the pit shooting dead each fresh fleeting installation of condemned persons. He acts on the imperative to work efficiently. He believes that once dirt covers the dead bodies, the pit will naturally become a grave. The grave's holdings will also disintegrate unbeknownst to the rest of the living. The surface of the ground can be resealed and made continuous again for him and his kin to live and work.

Are we surprised that the condemned prisoners do not scream in protest prior to their death?

Those ordered to enter the pit address those already shot with soothing words. Those facing their mortal death are proud to stand on the shoulders of their kin. It can be called miraculous that the dead ones remain standing. The executioner considers this fact as an outcome of his good and thoughtful planning. There will be a smaller area for him to conceal.

One condemned man giggles with another when the latter explains to his younger sister that the executioner is afraid of earthworms. "The poor idiot wastes so much ammunition because he doesn't know which end to shoot first or when the animal is actually dead!"

It Comes with the Job

It comes with the job. Cleaning up other people's vomit: all that has someone's unintelligible signature on it: a smell, a color, the evocation of a bad trip, a prolonged ache, or an impossible to rectify negligence—convulsions from bottled up spirits or the un-twisting torque of myco-hallucinogens. I wipe away the wall paintings, the post action display, the two-hour spills, the five-second eruption, the half-second punch. I pop back the line of rhythmic dents or pot-marks and poke-throughs. I scratch and scratch and we scratch at whatever they wrote: waxy testimonials, errors, numbered pronouns, a stated message beside another stated message beside another.

And then I gather what they could not hold: moist confetti drawn into the sky: an attractive image—nothing more—soon garbage to be, and scrape it off my tools into the collective bin.

Viewfinder

It is a warm sunny midsummer day. Without plan or destination I go street walking. Downtown East New York everyone is selling supplies on the street. This is no quaint rural scene of an old woman with dried apricot cheeks offering us tarnished silverware and dainty tea sets. I think I must be in India. . . Some of the junk could be stolen, or looted from abandoned apartments, or arranged to look like it all came from "my own closet" even though it was picked out and collected from more than one hundred eviscerated trash bags. These are not moving out sales because there is nowhere to go. We are not talking about someone selling apartment furnishings; the apartment is long gone.

On that corner is a rack of clothing that looks as though it was ripped off the backs of boy and girl punks banging around in a late night club. The sequin tunics with tattered hems are stained with wine, sweat and rain. Just find me the right girl whose boy is the right mixture of virility and filth and these clothes will be ready to go at it again, straightaway, tonight even.

The open-air bazaar is vulnerable to the weather—if the rain starts pouring down, turning old magazines into paper pulp, or a strong wind knocks the mirrored bathroom cabinet into the fluted oil and vinegar set, cracking the former and shattering the latter, and the whipping wet gust drags those fur trousers into the gutter runoff, then so be it. The one in charge can leave it all behind and walk away. He can tuck himself into the local donut shop until the next sunny day arrives.

On most days, I tell myself not to look down because I find the scene unavoidably distracting. The sidewalk is littered with so much insoluble detail that is better not seen.

What do I mean by insoluble detail? When I walk, I am working; I am cleaning the spaces between my teeth and peeling away the opaque film residues that develop when one follows any stubborn daily routine. I am looking for new ideas. To do so, I scour the streets; hanging suspended beside teeming intersections, I take a rest feeling at home in my own private encyclopedia. My surroundings have to be subdued in order that I can hear myself think. The fact that every one of those objects laid out on the sidewalk is chattering away about its own pitiable life history simply drowns out my thoughts. I lose the thread.

Except this one time, this warm sunny day when I spot a black piece of plastic between a jeweled pillbox and a wrinkled pair of pink satin shoes. Although somehow unidentifiable, I guess the thing is the viewfinder broken off from a toy gun. It costs me a quarter. Then it is in my hands, bought and mine. I'm empowered by the thing. Within minutes I become a cameraman who needs only the right angle to capture the world in perfectly lyrical vignettes. I am making studies for my next film, to seal my future career as the great filmmaker. This key piece of hardware is enough. I can study people the way I have always wanted to. I cut them into select fragments, nice erotic bulges and squinting eyes. I zoom into their private places, hiding behind my device and then twirl away if they become too suspicious . . . I mean if I see my own image reflected in their questioning faces.

I take on Broadway. The whistling core samples the crowd, filling my eyes with the rich detail. A dark face turns into the sun. I work quickly to suck its sudden brightness up through the tube. I place myself close enough and track only one detail of the face at a time. The mouth is smiling. The face belongs to him. He is set into the crowd, traveling with the unending throng along the street. He has arms, and like a playful cat, he swipes at the viewfinder. He wants to know what it is. Through my little tube I draw him out of the crowd.

Sailing down Broadway, we turn left on Bleeker. He starts to act. He poses. He imitates and even anticipates my directions. He is still smiling. Then I forget about the others, about my independence, and follow him.

Circling each other like dogs do, we advance. We take on new terrain, climbing over a chainlink fence and into a playground.

I swim in the sandbox and he follows. He throws himself down the slide and I squat to catch him in my hollow barrel. I am excited and impressed, believing in the possible and wanting to go on. The afternoon is falling when he takes the little toy in his own hands. There is no more sun and I think to go home. Fear comes with the night.

I'm now trapped in his sight line and he in mine. And upon the game's end, the lines splinter into place and possible—specified, but uncertain, and in the end fallacious, histories. As it is getting late and we are finally feeling our weight and our way, we drag one another into the almost secluded apartment foyer. It is an extra-tempting address for the necessary movements to arrive at the glorious mysteries. Below the panel of brass bells, and the sulfurous glow of lamplight, between the four doors and atop the dark and light tiled floor, he tears into my fur cap with a slender build and gentle fingers.

Strange, but I remember him always clothed, and only I began tunneling into song, lying on my back, throbbing and pressed against a corner of that little room.

He told me where he lived. I traveled there on another day, but found no place to match the address. I was close to the West River; the street was wide and I was vaguely sad that this unverifiable relation would never be repeated.

Sequence

After he had already died, his father brought me to the train station. His father is now also dead. I haven't yet returned to my friend's home again so I don't need to know who would drive me to the train station. If I did return, I imagine his younger brother would drive me in the family car, hold my hand for a moment when we step outside and say goodbye in the name of his father and his brother whom I loved.

Heavenly Bodies

I must admit I become actually anxious for those who have little footing. I am a light weight. I have simply learned that I am capable of several postures, and that I possess the exceptional ability to assume for a sufficiently short duration the weight balance of another individual even in her absence.

My grandmother was inclined to lend me her keys whenever she traveled. I would feed the cat and the apartment was then mine to stew and lounge in. Her apartment was sunken one-half story below ground and was always therefore cool and damp. As the only window faced west, the room rarely, if ever, was struck with direct sunlight. These physical characteristics as well as the yellowing walls and muddy colors of the two oil paintings she attached to the walls helped me enormously.

Of several darkly colored pieces of furniture, my grandmother had a low-sitting, well-padded armchair in which she would sit for long stretches at a time knitting, sewing, or reading while she listened to the radio. As the seat was so low to the floor, she could raise herself up only with difficulty and much effort.

Normally she was in her armchair when I came for one of my regular visits. This time, in her absence, I sat in my usual station on the bed. The cat was of course collecting dust on the windowsill and I found myself staring at the vacant armchair.

Slowly, I got up and lowered myself into it with the same steady exertion as my grandmother. I let my feet rest on the floor; my feet parallel and slightly spread apart. Then I waited until her weight and immobility entered my young legs.

For as long as I had known her, my grandmother had swollen legs and feet. She wore thick and shiny nylons, a special model for older women susceptible to thrombosis. She stuck her feet into black suede orthopedic shoes that in combination with the shine from her stockings gave the lower half of the body the appearance of a large plastic doll.

Her legs were rigid. I am not suggesting that she was inactive. I can recall no image of my grandmother sitting with crossed legs, for example, or raising her arms above her head to change a light bulb, or to pluck a peach off from a sagging, low-lying tree branch. If the something she was handling fell to the floor, it was usually one of us who picked it up. Perhaps we jumped to help her, just to avoid the strange sight of the bending down and the skirt of her dress making a scratchy sound as it slid up across her shiny nylons.

In order to describe what I feel demands courage. I can describe a grainy feeling. It seemed as if my undersoles flattened out and expanded horizontally. I could no longer distinguish my foot from the floor, nor could I, and nor did I want to raise my foot in the air. I knew something was in process and must not be disturbed.

I had discerned then, it had seemed quite natural then, that I touched the ground.

The Face

If I am capable of making a face just as I am becoming dead all over, it should be goggle-eyed, with the mouth stretched beyond a smile until at each corner a pit-shaped opening appears such that my face, at the very least, expresses surprise.

The Daughter Wakes Up From the Dream of Emerging from Her Father's Head

With the site's surface entirely gridded, the architect can perform an act of extrusion. It makes a familiar sound—a comical aural chiche—of an in and upward suck—volumes popping up from the bare patch of sloped or level ground. This is how we build, up from the ground, and across the colored plane.

That this is the way it happens is not problematic. This is not a problematic procedure. It has happened, it will happen and we all understand how it can happen.

The corollary is a different matter: i.e. when the thing falls out of the sky—and lands—we have to simply scratch our heads—to chuckle at how sometimes the delicately maintained comic balance is upset: an imagined image itself becomes comic as an isolated vision or a cartoon. We smile in our complacent understanding of how it might be possible that a procedure can also undergo convulsions just as sometimes happens to the individual.

As the story goes, the man composes with preconceived volumes, and I do mean preconceived. The four more-or-less platonic volumes we all know balanced on his fingertips before being placed on the X of his dominion.

He lies down; he is resting or dreaming the lay of the land. He is pressed forward and upward by a gentle push from below. He looks around, turning his head as far as it will go, to the left and to the right. There is a smell of foliage in the air. What he sees, and it is a far distance which falls within his view, is breathtaking . . .

The Head

The head of an adult has a different feel than that of a child. A child moves his head very freely and often; he shakes, tilts it side to side, nods front and back—and even uses his head to charge at someone with whom he is angry.

The adult moves his head slowly. He holds it with a studied stillness that sends a message of focus, difficulty, and concentration. He owns his head. He owns it with a hard-earned arrogance that knows its unbearable weight. And if you touch this possession even in a gesture of careless affection or simply carelessly—that matured adult might turn on you. You might also feel like washing your hands right away. Even if the head you just handled didn't stink or feel sweaty—you'll still need to rinse off the memory of intimacy that coats your fingertips.

I have touched a child's head a million times and nonetheless have barely any outstanding tactile memories of it. I do remember holding a newborn's head in the palm of the hand: it's warm, fuzzy and uneven.

I remember once approaching a curly black-haired head, bent down among a group of children who were resting on the ground after a tiresome tour of my large house—it's a kind of inherited museum, you see. I was standing when I patted the top and let my fingers sink into her curls. The head turned slowly upwards and I knew instantly, but still too late, that I had just mistakenly patted the head of an adult. She wasn't smiling. My eyes traveled down, recognizing the swell of her breasts and the slightly awkward position of her bent legs. She no longer blended in that field of shifting little heads.

The Belly of a Bird

He ran the bath, sitting on the toilet as the water rushed out of the faucet. All day, Javier had washed the cook's tools—large encrusted pots that banged against the thin metal walls of the sink. For a while the room's brightness kept him awake. He dozed, woke, stopped the water flow and undressed. His body felt limp, energy-less, except for a tight knot of exhaustion in his gut where a seed of despair nested, swollen and turgid. He broke into the bath, sliding his body under until the water's surface met the soft underside of his chin. He soaked. Fastening his fingers tightly around a floating bar of soap, he rubbed it across his chest and down each arm building up a creamy lather. He tried to alleviate an itch at the side of his nose with a quick movement by his shoulder but a bit of lather snuck up his nostrils and caused him to cough. The smell floated up from the pot, from the cloudy water, and from his hands. The smell stuck to his forearms and hovered like an odious cloud around his face and neck. He worked up a lather; it was something like washing a poodle. He had to skin the dog: to shave its coat. He had to—it was a kind of ritual of survival, if not daily then every couple of days: at least weekly.

Bringing his body to rise up to the surface, he watched as his curly pubic hair sprouted into the suds. He found this image attractive, and gently parted the hairs to make a path for his fingers. But his bottom fell quickly down to the hard base of the tub. The soapy water welled up and splashed sending waves from side to side.

Ay! Mamacita! And it was becoming difficult to use his body, to enjoy the use of his body. And it was difficult to move, and not to move. He had tried to bring all of himself to love her, to lift her on top and to rock her against his hips. Voluntarily she had straddled his waist; even if, at first, he lay there, immobile, she had known how to be patient, how to use the warmth and moisture that her body exuded. They met in the bed: sometimes, when they were able . . . when he was able. Then they slept together between the sheets, breathing in the air of mingled temperatures, breathing in something of each other: that which rests, and resting, rises and blends with its neighbor. He sat up, washed his genitals and rubbed his feet, picking away the dirt between his toes. Finally he stretched out and let the back of his head drop into the water.

Javier woke up—swollen to a point of bursting. It must have been the weariness he had felt in the evening. He couldn't move. He just lay there, stuck in the bed, discovering himself swollen like a seed about to release its primary root, dependent on sun and rain for further encouragement. It was the days that moved him. Monday, conscious till its end, had carried him to Tuesday . . .

The cook set three white empty five-gallon stewed tomato containers on the floor besides the large stove.

"Javier, get over here! Help me with this."

Each secured a grip on one of the handles of the big steel pot and sent a thick rush of chicken broth pouring into the first of the containers. It filled up too fast. They rocked the pot back just in time. Still, a yellow piece of something had plopped into the broth splashing soup onto Javier's white pants. They were more cautious in filling the second container and by the third, pieces of onion, chicken meat and white bits of cartilage clung to the side of the empty pot. "Stick this in the sink," said the cook. Javier lifted it up and carried it over just as the cook said and walked back rolling up his sleeves.

"Go get a top to close this one or we'll be swimming in soup all day. I want you to bring these to the walk-in and leave them by the door. Get out three bags of chicken then come back over here fast — we have a lot to do."

Javier slipped the edge of his palms under the lip of one of the containers and lifted. The sharp edge cut into his skin and his forearms bulged under the strain. Halfway there, he set the bucket down, straightened up, stretched his hands, and rubbed his arms.

The pale yellow liquid in the second one with no cover sloshed back and forth. Midway, some soup jumped over the edge and made a wide wet spot across Javier's belly. Some more splashed onto the floor. His effort spent on lifting the container up while walking, Javier couldn't avoid stepping through the little puddle. The second set beside the first, he returned for the third.

"Where are my chickens? You're too slow. Come on, move—"

Turning back the door, Javier was met with the standing smell of refrigerated meat. He moved the white containers with their lively contents carefully to the other side: into that dank cool room. He stepped out, closed the thick insulated door and, remembering the chickens, used all his weight to pull back the long handle again until he heard its big click of acceptance. Marking the place of the three containers he had just brought to rest to the right of the entry, he searched into the chilled darkness of the little room for the clear plastic bags tightly packed with the white to yellow skinned chickens. He found them resting on the floor. Parts bulging, parts retreating, other parts showing themselves with only a fingerlike tip on the bag's taut surface while the rest was hidden deep inside. One bag leaned against another and a third and fourth were in a huddle beside the filigree stack of cardboard trays holding pint sized containers of sour cream.

Javier dragged the three bags of chickens out of the cooler. Before heading back he rubbed the chill away from his hands and arms. He patted his thighs. He hoisted the cold weight of one onto his shoulder and lifted another. The cook was leaning his weight on the countertop, busy writing down something with a stubby pencil.

Javier stood at the sink. With a bit of fingernail, he picked at the caulk ring at the base of the faucet. He grabbed the bottle of dish soap and drew a circle around the inside of the pot. He lifted the pot back out of the sink onto the floor and leaned over. With full arm movements, he built up a rich lather, occasionally stopping to scrape at bits of food glued to the sides. Instead of lifting the pot back into the sink—he attached a pink hose into the spigot guiding its free end into the pot. He turned on the hot water full blast, distributing the stream across the surface to bring down the suds. Bending at the knees, he grunted as he heaved the full pot up and against the sink edge to empty it. He repeated the whole sequence and brought the clean pot to the aluminum shelves set up to the right beside the cook's stove. Javier returned to the sink, undid the clasp around one of the bags and let the chickens tumble into the sink. He rinsed each individually, filling its hollow with water and rubbing its loose sticky skin under the cool stream. Leaving one sink full with wet chickens, Javier hooked several on his fingers and carried them over to the prep counter. He prepared his station: retrieving the proper knives, sorting bowls and wiping down the chopping block.

Just as he was about to make the first incision, the cook, with his intrusive body, stopped Javier, knife raised, and substituted himself for still another demonstration.

The cook had a round pudgy head covered evenly with a blond to silvery grey stubble. As a fruit he would unquestionably be a peach: a large one, slightly bruised at the temples. Days of staring through aromatic steam and his afternoon glass of Pernod had given him watery eyes with a dartlike look that pierced through the accumulated moisture.

"Last time, Javier, there were too many rough edges—rough edges means more scum to skim during the cooking, and a muddier taste . . . *comprende*? Watch me, and pay attention."

Pulling away one of the legs by the narrow neck of the drumstick, the cook split the taut curve of skin with the tip of the slender knife. He momentarily moved the leg in and out, operating the hinge before shearing it off cleanly between ball and socket. He turned the cut side towards Javier to indicate the cut's smooth precision before repeating the same action on the chicken's other leg and similarly, the wings.

"Let's go over the removal of the breast once again—take this cleaver here. Sit the chicken on the block and then hit her with a clean strong swing."

The cleaver came down, and everything resting on the counter hopped up as the wide blade met the wood surface.

See that? Put the breast with the legs and chop the back into two or three pieces. Hand me another one.

The cook demonstrated his technique again, and then once more before handing the cleaver to Javier.

Picking up a stranded piece of creamy brown material from the counter and holding it delicately between his fingers the cook said, "Javier, I want all the livers and the giblets. Try not to break them. Remove the fat carefully with a very sharp knife and cut away this stringy stuff. After you've done just what I have shown you with 20 plus, come back to me and we'll go over the next step."

The cook wiped his fingers on his apron and walked through the double doors into the dining room taking with him that smell . . . of sweat, blood and liquor, of flaky scalp and unwashed sleep.

With each successive chicken that Javier brought onto the counter, it was impossible for him not to refer to the cook's exemplary demonstration. Javier timidly maneuvered the chicken leg back and forth in order to better reveal the position of the hidden joint.

He drew his blade across the skin, through the flesh and the white cartilage, and the leg fell away cleanly except for a stubborn piece of skin that had to be sawed through and pulled. He moved to the second leg, to the wings and to the successive cracks of the slender ribs as the cleaver broke though. It took time to cut up twenty chickens. Javier lost count but relaxed with a smile to discover the simple trick that he need only count the legs and divide by two. He noticed the slippery numb feeling of his fingers: something partially hardened rubbed off and was being massaged into his skin; by the 18th, his fingers began to stick to the gluey translucent flesh. At his back, the dishwasher's spray was busy rinsing off the remaining bits of food and sauce before the next batch of plates and cups were slipped into place. Triggered by the continuous sound of spraying water, Javier felt the urgent need to relieve himself. He left his station, holding his unwashed hands at a slight distance from his body and dropping his head as he passed through the double doors, dreading another encounter with the cook.

The cook was sitting with the bartender, smoking and twirling the ice in his glass. He didn't look up as Javier passed their table.

The door to the women's bathroom was propped open. Teresa and two other waitresses were standing intertwined in front of the mirror. They weren't really touching; it was just that the room was so small; they managed to overlap in such a way that each girl could have her piece of the mirror to apply her makeup. The girls ignored him, concentrating with widely opened eyes on the smooth spread of creamy color on the lips, the eyelids and the upper curve of the cheeks. Javier, clothed in white, spotted with food stains, greased, and a still unappetizing precursor to any number of dishes, stood there for the slightest moment, his mouth hung open, his eyes curious and then again dull until he was sure that they noticed him. Until he could sense himself, as he was seen: clothed in white, hands held palms upward in front of his body, with an unloved head popping out at the neck of his white T-shirt;

"What are you staring at!" It was Teresa who spoke, without turning to him, watching instead her lips move in the mirrored reflection.

He was relieved to close the door behind him, to urinate, and to pull up his pants quickly, energetically, refreshed. As he passed through the dining room, the three women were already working the floor, Teresa was leaning at the bar, her heeled shoe rocking back and forth on the rod that served as a foot rest at the base of the bar.

The cook was at his station, doing Javier's work: finishing up the remaining chickens. Beside the counter on the floor was a large sack of onions and two empty white containers.

"I've finished up for you. There are 22 chickens. Wash this at the sink and come back. I will need 33 onions peeled and quartered. The livers look awful; What the hell did you do? You didn't follow what I said. Did you? Livers can't be pulled apart. To do it right, your knife has got to be sharp enough. No ripping. Remember, never pull livers apart."

"Javier, you say you had a couple of kids?"

"No, it wasn't me."

"But you're married, right?"

"Not any more."

"Hey—I'm sorry. But, when you first started working here you were still with her—wasn't her name Yolanda, or Sabrina—or am I wrong?"

"Sabrina."

"Well, the reason I ask is that my daughter is just about to have a baby, and my wife is looking for someone to help around the house after the kid's born—and I thought you might know somebody."

At first Javier resisted—but he couldn't help himself from imagining Sabrina in the cook's daughter's house picking up baby rattles and teddy bears from the shiny wood floor and then stacking last night's dinner plates and this morning's coffee mugs methodically in the dishwasher. There in the kitchen keeping her company is the baby herself. It's time to feed and she spoons beige mud into the mouth of the fat white baby. Sabrina wears dark clothes, and seldom smiles. When Javier rings the bell, she abruptly drops the spoon and the cereal splatters. She runs out the front door and begins hitting the elevator button with a desperate urgency.

Javier's thoughts were pierced by the rising smell of onion; his eyes started to water.

As he waited for the cook, hip against counter, the work area laid out with small open jars filled with spices, larger bowls filled half-way with chopped herbs, wet livers, white flour, and beside the stove, two large empty bowls, Javier lowered two fingers into the one with green peppercorns. He crushed a couple of miniature globes between thumbnail and forefinger, brought the finger up to his nose and then finally wiped it clean across his tongue. With the padded round of his middle finger he teased the shiny surface of the raw livers, and dusted his tongue with a few grains of cayenne. He noticed the small flask of brandy at the end of the row of bowls and was about to reach for it when he was interrupted by the cook.

"Set two pots up to boil in the back and then the double boiler. The béchamel is in the cooler. Make sure all the skillets are clean. Check today's menu. Everything should be ready—I really shouldn't have to tell you."

Later on, while sitting on an overturned bucket, peeling potatoes, he saw himself pouring a handful of green peppercorns into a pan of bubbling butter. He lay down the floured livers and shook the pan from side to side. He carefully flipped each cluster with a wooden spatula. He breathed in the aroma and listened prognostically to the popping in the pan. At the right moment he would add a pinch of cayenne, salt and pepper and a splash of brandy, or tequila? He'd wait for a brown crust to appear before turning the Sautéed Livers with Green Peppercorns out onto a large plate. Before serving he'd garnish the dish with several sprigs of fresh red currants . . .

There was a delivery: a half pound of dried mint in a brown paper bag tossed on top of the five gallon container of yogurt just at the height of Javier's nose. He breathed in the smell of the mint, his forearms becoming chilled strapped around the heavy refrigerated container.

At around five thirty, Jose, the dishwasher, tapped Javier lightly on the shoulder. He made a pointing gesture with his head and walked slowly to the double doors, popping up his hip with each step in his version of a street cool gait. Javier released his grip on the knife he had been using, its blade securely wedged into a large onion, and followed. Javier and Jose and two other men in white sat around the round table positioned nearest to the kitchen. The cook emerged bearing two large platters: one heaped with baked chicken legs and the other with rice. Teresa brought everyone Cokes from the bar. The cook lit a cigarette and offered one to Teresa. As the cook and Teresa smoked, the men ate. Before finishing his cigarette, the cook rose, turned to Javier and said, "I'll need you in 10 minutes Javier, hmm?"

Javier, now full, watched as Jose picked his teeth. He especially had his eye on one tooth that was wrapped in gold only at the edges—the center remaining white and uncapped. There was no conversation. Javier pushed his plate away and almost as an afterthought collected all the dishes to bring into the kitchen.

Before the evening guests started to arrive in substantial numbers, Javier replenished the cook's palette of prep bowls, bottles and trays of ingredients and removed dirty, dripping, mismatched or stained empties, returning them full to the proper location.

He stood at the counter preparing to shadow the cook's every move.

In the rectangular aluminum pan pieces of pork, all of a layer veined with white fat but lean and glistening, waited until three of the cook's round trimmed fingers and a thumb below lifted each up—one, two, three—to place them in bubbly butter. He slipped a lollipop-sized plop of oil into the skillet to delay the butter's browning, eyed the pot sitting on the back burner and its healthy steaming, smelling with question the hidden greens doneness. All ready now for flipping, for salt and black pepper, the steaks quizzed the cook to evoke names of the invited: thyme and tarragon, but walk by basil, and up to the bowl where lilies are floating. Tilt it over, drain the water, and transfer the swollen porcini into the pan. Simmer—drain out the water—drop out the greens and pinch off a leaf, test nibble for doneness. He returned to the skillet to finish the bed. He sprinkled in flour and uncorked a generous pour of wine—stirring all the while—eyeing the plate, eyeing his help, Javier, to suggest the man come forth with simple readiness. The sauce thickened and clung to the spoon. The cook lifted that skillet from the burner, tilted it, coaxing the sauce to blanket the plate. With overbearing concentration he arranged the medallions in a centered ring and painted the meat with the remaining dregs of the sauce. An altogether different touch dropped threads of orange rind, crisscross fashion, in the middle of the plate. As always, some sauce jumped its boundary and splattered on the plate's shiny white rim, and the cook, not yet exhausted, used a corner of his apron to wipe the distracting blotch away. With a short shove to its rim, the cook motioned that Javier should transfer the dish to the pick-up counter.

In its current condition, the dish looked more like a still life painting than a hot, nourishing meal. As Javier brought the dish to pick-up, he couldn't help from wondering if the sauce was even still warm after all the time the cook had spent in arranging the elements on the plate. He eased his thumb in, covering its tip with a cap of the rich brown sauce. When he lay down the plate and withdrew his hand, a thick line of sauce crossed over into the plate's clean white rim—interrupting the frame. His face broke into smiles. Teresa picked up the dish, swished out onto the floor and over to the proper table. Thumb in mouth, the sauce slid over his tongue. Although no longer hot, it had a warm earthy taste, the orange peel there as a reminder that things that grow upward in brightly colored fullness do fall back to the ground.

With the sweet, smoky but still fetid taste of the mushrooms came the memory of the tree. Under the tree's exposed roots, the mushrooms had been hiding their little heads. Above hung the fruit: bright orange globes shining in the late afternoon sun, able, as they fell, to lace the scent that perfumed the air into the plane of the earth. A seated man, his back against the tree trunk, breaks open his packed lunch in the dappled shade of the tree's branches. The sun creeps through, warms the sliced meat, making it sweat its fat, and brings out his beer's yeasty flavor. Work once again calling, the man leaves the remains of his lunch: multicolored bits that now speckle the ground will darken and decay in a number of days. The sun sets, the orange's fullness flattens into blue-black rounds pinned against the evening sky. Evening's earth: an animal's bed, tilled under hoof, rolled in and shaken off—a dusting—a second skin in which to settle.

Javier woke to the kitchen's smooth metal surfaces and crème tiled walls.

The next order, the next after that, and the third, too, lay on the aluminum counter.

Already as the first dish had been sent away, beads of sweat surfaced on the cook's forehead. He picked out the first piece of paper, read out the news and barked the plan.

"Javier, four pork chops. You're doing the side: Pasta with Leek sauce. Eight minutes."

After tossing a small bundle of leeks into one of three simmering pots of boiling water, Javier picked out two steel bowls, a smaller and a larger and ran over to the cooler feeling ridiculous for running in such tight quarters. He pulled a good handful of pasta, the pork chops, and four containers of crème frâiche and rushed back to the stove. The leeks had begun to look like water plants, more transparent and with a richer green color. He lay the chops on the cook's counter. The cook transferred the meat to the prepared pan where it was received with a popping sound followed by a continuous sizzling. Javier drained the leeks, threw the pasta into a second pot of boiling water and lined up the hot wet leeks on the counter to be sliced. Pasta cooking, oven door opening, hot air hitting legs, steaming knees . . . drain the pasta. And the cheese? Javier had to jostle a cramped head. Where is the cheese? Ask the cook? Ask!

"Cheese is in the small fridge, Javier, always in the small fridge. Don't think, just move. Hurry—grate, grate and stir it in—fast!"

The cook pulled the readied plate toward himself, staring nervously at the browning meat. By now, the cook was prodding Javier from the back. As if in involuntary protest, Javier's movements became wooden and impossibly slow. He let himself be angrily pushed aside giving the cook clear access to the leeks waiting on the board. The cook sliced with an accelerated rhythm shouting, "Drain the damn noodles! Idiot!"

In his stunned state, Javier could still do as he was told. He returned with a dripping colander, which he emptied into the waiting bowl. The cook slid the leeks into the béchamel and stirred. After placing two pork chops on each plate, the cook forked a tangle of pasta onto each plate and topped each with a spread of the sauce.

"Parsley, said the cook," and waved the plates away.

Each time Javier felt humiliated, he would steal. The first moment he was alone, he stuffed two raw squabs behind his shirt and apron. One slid down into his underpants and clawed at him like a female hand complete with sharp nails. He hid the squabs in his locker in a plastic bag hung between his slacks and shirt.

Sunday it was the birds, Tuesday, the kumquats and a fatty piece of Virginia ham, Thursday, an ear of ginger and two star anise, Thursday night, a jar of black truffle paste, a handful of new potatoes, and a few sprigs of parsley. Early Friday morning, before the cook had even arrived, he took a pint of red currants and a jar of lingonberries, imported from Sweden. Last month it was equipment: a small, sharp paring knife, a special thick and curved needle for suturing birds and several skewers. Each night, Javier unpacked the stolen food in the dark of his small kitchen. He stored those things needing refrigeration safely in the fridge and the dry goods in one of his three nearly empty cabinets.

The restaurant "Bon Jour" was set in the middle of the block. Pushing out through the swinging glass doors, Javier paused at the curb and the smell caught up with him, encircling him from behind. He had wanted to cross quickly, but the rush of cars forced him to wait. Javier rubbed his eyes and instinctively brought his fingers up to his nose. There it was, just under the skin: the faintly bloody and slightly rotting smell from all of those raw chickens. Javier looked down at his shoes: two boxy steel-toed boots with a dull shine, part animal part mineral, that glimmered in the cool lamplight. He scraped his soles against the edge of the curb. Finally there was a long enough pause in the flow; he rushed himself, already hearing the train's rumble. The doors opened and he swung into a seat, the plastic bag of ingredients hitting the seat beside his.

Javier lived in apartment 5D all the way at the end of the mustard and pumpkin colored hallway. He walked step by step past the many doors, drunk with exhaustion, and nearly banged into the end wall. Javier slid in the key, cradling the rest in his hand to prevent them from jangling. He slipped out of his shoes, and peeled off his socks. He hadn't yet felt the need to flick on the lights—his blank mind suspended in the still air of the entryway. Living room beyond—he continued ahead politely, softly, and sunk to the floor. Stretched out, head and shoulders against baseboard—Javier fell asleep. He woke up later—to quiet darkness—and steadied himself to his knees, disturbing the slew of magazines spread out on the coffee table. Feeling groggy and disoriented, he found his way to the bedroom. The bed bounced gently as he lay down.

His eyes opened onto a dark windowless room. The air was still and warm, and laced with his smell: something moist leaking from a pot of simmering cauliflower. Accustoming his eyes to the darkness, he made out the large and darker mass of the TV set. He fumbled for the controls.

"So what will you be showing us today?"

"It's a French dish that's very simple to prepare: Roulades de Porc, or translated—Pork Rolls."

"It sounds much tastier in French, doesn't it—(laughter)—and what's this here?"

"Here we have four slices of lean pork. It's a special cut that you won't find in the supermarket. Go to your butcher and tell him to cut it from the leg—thin and extra wide. And this is fresh fennel, which the Italians call *fin-o-chio*—it has a slightly licorice taste and should be bought firm and not yellowed. We'll be cooking with it today, but you can also eat it raw, like carrots and celery, with a fresh dip."

He switched the channel. Two voices were speaking over a shiny steel bowl filled with a glistening mixture of grey scallops, beaten egg, and finely chopped parsley. The camera followed the cook's well-scrubbed but hairy hands as he added a premeasured amount of clear amber liquid into the bowl, mixing it gently before sliding it into the mirror surface of a frying pan prepared with a small pool of melted butter. Then came the amplified sizzling sound and the deep inhaling of the pretty interviewer. Javier didn't care what dish they were preparing; he was interested in the chef's movements. How he used a spatula; and how he sliced, chopped and tossed the ingredients, scraping the underside of the mantle away from the metal surface of the pan. The pan shuttled on its burner, knocking against the grill.

Javier went to make a cup of coffee. He opened the fridge. It was nearly empty except for the pile of stolen booty on the middle shelf.

"Just a small squeeze of lemon just before serving will bring out the subtle taste of the scallops. Too much and that lovely flavor will remain hidden—and your friends will be complimenting you on that lemony dish. Voila!—Now, try it."

"Mmm, that's scrumptious. It's sooo subtle, I'll have to taste it again . . . (laughter)."

The doorbell buzzed. There it was, the smiling sphere of Yolanda's face balancing with a slight wobble on her buoyant rotund body. Her shiny black hair, streaked with white, was pulled back and greased into a small bun. Her extra-large bosom pushed out an orange cardigan.

"Ay Caríño!—Buenos días Javiercito, mi amor."

Her arms stretched out as two strong diagonals. She bobbed backwards and forwards, coming towards him with those ready arms to bind him to her secure body. She squeezed his ribs, patting the back of his head sharply with the edge of her hand. Instinctively, he dodged her advances, slipping out of reach by folding back upon himself. But energetic Yolanda bent her thick arm around his neck in an uncompromising head hold. He was lassoed! Numbness ebbing, his defenses tingling. He was unpleasantly surprised at first, angry even. She was smiling triumphantly, proud to be able to express her strength and affection at the same time.

"Javier, tu madre ha acabado de llamarme. Ella está demasiada preocupada—contigo—me entiendes? Yo no sé de na-da, y no he dicho na-da—" and with pursed lips: *"mm-mm."*

Yolanda's erect pointer finger gave emphasis to every syllable. She drew ornamental curves in the air, fingers landing on this or that part of his body.

Her hand rose higher as if she were about to land one on his shoulder or to perform a quick karate chop—just to make sure he was paying attention to the drama of it all.

"No, no, no. Javier. *Ella—tu madre no se comprende nada, nada de nada. Como, por ejemplo, su hijo, un hombre joven, vive. En-ton-ces, ella cree lo peor."*

With this last word, Yolanda broke into a nearly hysterical laughter—raised her hand and forcefully hit Javier on the chest.

"Vamos—bebamos un café!"

Javier was swept into a manageable pile, and led, prodded and pushed to Yolanda's front door. Once inside he breathed in the complex smell of meat stewed with onions, a flowery perfume with the odor of mentholatum on the horizon.

He sat at the table, in the kingdom of her kitchen, while she prepared the food. The refrigerator hummed; the coffee dripped into a shining glass pot. Her large body entirely blocked his view of the stove—the orange knit cardigan above a black pleated skirt shifting back and forth with a slight rotation. When she opened the refrigerator door, Javier caught a glimpse of an orderly and well-stocked interior. He listened to the eggs cracking one after the other: seven, eight, nine, ten but wouldn't dare protest the sheer quantity. He heard a whisk beating and the mixture sizzling in the hot pan. Yolanda suddenly turned around with a pan full of soft scrambled eggs.

"Cuánto? Aquí? Aquí?"

The wide edge of the spatula pressed into the mixture breaking off twice the amount he had consented to. Its blade disappeared and a glistening pile rose and slid onto his plate. Yolanda served herself an equally generous portion and sat down.

"Caríño, dame esta botella de salsa. Por favor."

She poured out enough sauce to cover the eggs and quickly got up to bring over the pot of coffee that had just quit its sputtering. She poured him a cupful and without asking spooned in two teaspoons of sugar and added two buttered rolls to an already full plate.

She lifted the coffee to her lips and smiling broadly, said,

"Bueno, come—come."

The eggs were delicious, creamy and scored with butter-filled crevasses. To his surprise, he had no difficulty finishing his portion.

Stilling her head's chewing movement for the first time since they had sat down, she leaned in, ready to insert a thermometer into what was once his little boy's bottom.

"Javier, dígame, como estás? Como te sientes? Dígame, cualquiera cosa—"

"*Tu madre se muere de preocupación!* Yeah! Mami is so worried for you."

"*Qué haces todo el tiempo, mi hijo?*"

"I'm just working."

There was a tourist's map of Florida taped carefully to the refrigerator. The wiggling brown border enclosed a golden yellow shape dotted with miniature cartoon illustrations of the best sightseeing attractions.

Javier could imagine his mother, a petite woman wearing a worried expression as an integral part of her identity, waking up in the Sunshine State. She'd do up her face with gaudy colors so she could be allowed to appear—live in one of those bubbles. If she could and if he'd take notice, she'd wave all day long even as she was doing her job, dancing to the same 20 seconds of music applied by the Tourist Bureau as equally emblematic.

Javier felt round and full. For the first time in ages he had been lovingly fed. He pushed his seat away from the table and very quietly, as if he were only correcting his posture said, "I'm also cooking—at home."

The apartment door slammed shut behind him. He lay down, full with food, in the dimly lit bedroom.

Tongue feels like a raw slab of pork. Pour the brandy over it and a white scum rises speckled with pepper, pepper through and through. But I can't taste anything—the ingredient's flavors are still held back by the chill of the fridge. It's time to light the fire and face the pan and the pan, the burner's range.

Javier's kitchen was windowless and small, its cabinets the color of old mannequins. The first recipe had the long title: Squab with Virginia Smoked Ham and Braised Fresh Kumquats. If he had a guest he would serve the dish with steamed string beans and new potatoes, finishing off the meal with a fresh baby escarole salad tossed with a simple vinaigrette.

Javier unwrapped the hard chunk of ham and placed it in the middle of his cutting board. He cut the ham into thin slices and then again, crosswise, making sure each piece had both meat and fat. He pulled out a saucer from the cabinet and gathered the chips of ham onto the plate. Javier got out his largest skillet. It landed on the stove with a bang. He got out the butter, the squab, and the kumquats from the refrigerator and set the ingredients in the right order around his cutting board. He lined up the salt shaker, the pepper grinder, a small bottle of brandy, and a box of matches beside the burner and uncorked the wine. A quarter cup each of the wine and the chicken stock found their place beside the other ingredients. Javier spooned three tablespoons of butter into the skillet and turned on the heat. As soon as it melted, he added the ham, the squab, the kumquats, salt and pepper. He watched the pan carefully, allowing the fruit and meat to brown. He added two tablespoons of brandy and torched the pan with a lit match. As soon as the flames died down, Javier poured in the cloudy purplish wine-chicken stock mixture and covered the pan. Javier brought the empty saucers and the measuring cup over to the sink. He folded the butcher paper that had held the squab and ham and tossed it in the garbage. Leaving only the salt and pepper, Javier wiped the counter down and readied a serving plate for the dish.

He made it a point to sample the different parts of the squab. He sucked on a bony wing; sliced a sliver of breast meat, and pulled away a muscle from the leg. He made a bite-size hole into the thigh and picked away a full bite from the animal's back. He gathered the strands of the rich dark meat and a couple pieces of the ham, piling both on a caramelized, candied, and braised kumquat and bit in. Javier stared at the uneaten portion. He got up abruptly and slid the rest into the flip-top garbage can. The open mouth snapped shut as soon as he released his foot.

Javier still had time. There was no need to go to bed yet. It's in the garbage. He pulled out a bag of popcorn and sat with the TV. Bed. Sleep.

The matte feel of the fresh mopped floor. The chairs still upturned: a hundred thin legs pointing up to the high ceiling. Coffee grinding. Bright whitewashed walls and ceilings chandeliered. Crossing the floor in brown punctually appearing caravans: foods arrived in boxes, in crates, in oversized brown bags, in Styrofoam, on lightweight trays. The wiry bartender bent at the waist then straightened as he set up his stand, clusters of glassware arrayed in his spread hands. The cook mouthed the day's strategy, pacing the dining room with the restaurant owner who was already eager to walk away. " . . . assuage with brown lentils . . . " Javier heard as he quietly and softly walked past the two men. He arrived at his locker and changed his clothes. Both in white, they met in the kitchen. They nodded. Eyeing if the objects were all in place, the cook turned to Javier.

"I want four gallons of chicken broth. Use the fryers in the cooler and save the flesh for the staff."

With paper, pencil and book, the cook exited through the dining room door.

Jose was showering a row of white plates. At his station, Javier peeled for twenty minutes, cut the vegetables for fifteen, and then handled the chickens, until it was all in the pot, boiling and then simmering. The kitchen was empty of people save for him and Jose. He stirred and the moist and savory air bloomed into his face.

He headed towards the dining room. They met at the double doors.

"What are you doing? I want you to prepare the lentils."

"Make enough for 10 to 12 orders—let's make that 20. 3 pounds of lentils, 15 cloves of garlic, a cup of olive oil and salt and pepper. After the lentils are done—and don't you dare overcook them—Let me know—I'll do the rest."

While he was standing at the counter, slipping the flesh off the boiled chickens—it came off so easily, just had to push at it with your fingertips, and oops, it slipped off, and all that fancy cutting technique was thoroughly unnecessary, the bird just gave it away— he saw a movement in the hollow carcass. It drew his fingers in. They scooped into the shadow and curled into a fist.

It came from all of them . . . the hooded hollows of the raw chickens . . . the nicely browned animal sitting still in a pool of burgundy-colored sauce . . . and just now the way the flesh slipped off with just a gentle prod of the finger: no fancy cutting, no cracking sound, just a push and a voluntary slide. It was while he was already sitting in the subway car that he allowed himself to develop the dish, to sink into his reverie; he brought it back. He felt it with his tongue and it made his eyes pop out. He was reeling . . . stolen flavors strung a beaded contour around a bell of alarm. The ingredients had now lost their specific reverberation amidst the louder stuttering ring.

Javier taught himself how to bone fowl. He practiced with small fryers he bought at the local supermarket. He first tried a technique that employed a neck-to-tail incision along the bird's backbone. After cutting away the skeleton, the body resembled a buttonless overcoat. Javier prepared a chestnut-liver stuffing, spooning the sticky mix onto the ragged mantle. Sewing the bird back into shape was difficult and disturbing. It took twenty minutes of perseverance. Javier bit at his bottom lip to dispel his desire to bake the bird unstitched.

He tried another boning technique that involved peeling the flesh back from the carcass without making any incisions whatsoever. This technique kept the chicken intact. He would only need to sew the opening at tail and neck.

Inside: a spiral.

He thought about a yeast bread dough spread with black truffle paste and then rolled. He got the idea from reading some recipes for the Chinese steamed buns called "Bao-Bao." The bread was so white and airy. Ideally, the elastic dough should carry up the fallen crest as it rose. The bird's empty cavity, perforated throughout with skin punctures inflicted by a skewer, should act like an oven, a steamer, or a pressure cooker. There was that drama of opposing forces: the bread dough's propensity to rise vs. the downward force from the weight of the bird's flesh. But perhaps the dough would be unable to push up the bird's breast. Forced to find the room to expand it might end up squeezing through the widely spaced stitches at the neck and tail.

Javier sharpened his knife. He tested the edge against his finger and then sharpened it a bit more. Javier sat the bird tail down on the counter and gently peeled back its skin, exposing the shoulder muscles. He felt around the fleshy opening below the absent neck for the wishbone. He drew the tip of his knife along bone's edge, cutting just deep enough that the thin bone could be plucked away from the bird's body. He scraped away the flesh covering the prominent wing joint, and sliced through tough white ligaments attaching wing to shoulder. The wing dropped free. He felt down along the collarbone, pushing up from below, to reveal its attachment to the breast bone. Placing his finger directly below the joint and applying a firm pressure he broke it open with a snap without using his knife. He pulled on the shoulder joint and the thin blade of a bone slipped out of its flesh bed. His fingers burrowed deeper into the bird's body, separating flesh from bony hull. In his ears, the sound of sticky layers separating and the clicking of fingertips in and out of moist flank. He was turning the bird inside out, its flesh cloak gathering at the ankles. The carcass stuck out like an upturned boat. Javier's fingers reached the thigh joint and with the tip of his knife, he carefully cut the leg loose. To free breast from bone, Javier slipped his knife into the ribcage and scored a line around the elongated cartilaginous flange of the breast bone. He could now lift the carcass away and cut through its last point of attachment at the animal's abbreviated tail.

He put the boned bird to the side and readied the squared pieces of pork filet. With repeated strikes from a mallet he thinned and flattened each filet, coaxing it to spread evenly into a thin still rectangular layer. He squeezed the sausages out of their skins and spooned several tablespoons of black truffle paste into the bowl. He dug in with his fingers, making a squelching sound as he mixed the two ingredients together, until the mixture turned a mottled blackish color. He seasoned with salt, pepper and thyme and hesitated for only a moment before tasting the raw mixture. He spread it as evenly as possible across the pork layer and carefully rolled the pink into black, sewing the loose pink edge to the roll. Filled with the roll, the bird took form. Javier sewed the neck and tail hole closed.

In a small skillet, Javier melted a piece of butter. He added the pigeon giblets and sautéed gently for a few minutes, seasoning the mixture with salt and pepper. Javier was working carefully; he took a deep breath to make sure he had the strength and concentration for the next steps. He added a good tablespoon of brandy to the giblets as well as a half cup of chicken stock and a quarter cup red wine, and let the mixture simmer. Javier transferred the liver, heart, and giblets from the broth to his blender and puréed them, slowly adding the fluid in a steady stream. The bird's innards were transformed into a smooth rich sauce.

After sliding small bits of butter under the skin, and sprinkling with coarse salt and freshly ground pepper, Javier slid the bird under the broiler. It baked, bubbled, and popped and Javier cleaned. He cleared the counters and swept the floor. He drank a cool glass of tap water. At the right moment, the grill slid out smoothly along its track. The tray below caught the reddish brown drippings fixed under a glistening layer of golden fat.

Under the broiler's flame, the bird's skin had become crisp, shiny and the color of dark honey. Its body was now full and firm. With a growing sense of pride, he drew the body off the grill and set it down on a clean cutting board. His movements were slow and deliberate, and as far as possible broken down into discrete steps. Holding the knife with a firm grip, he sliced the stuffed bird crosswise halfway down its middle section. The cut was clean and the knife free from any detached bits. Full of expectation, he separated the two halves. He turned each piece away from the other to expose the cut face. It was there, plainer to see than he had even imagined. He stood immobile, marveling that it now actually existed. After warming in a small saucepan, Javier covered the base of a large plate with the sauce. With trembling hands, he arranged the two halves on the prepared plate, the spiral sections turned on axis approximately 90°. He garnished the dish with a sprig of mint and a cluster of well-ripened red currants. He carried the plate ceremoniously to the small kitchen table, sat down and gazed at the dish. The lovely aroma started to have its effect. Javier sliced off a bite complete with crispy skin, tender pork and savory filling, dragging it through the opaque sauce and lifting the forkful to his mouth. After fully savoring all the flavors, he rolled out the name of the dish, Spiral . . . in . . . a . . . Squab. Javier continued to eat bite after bite, until there was nothing left but the berries and the leaves. He ate the former and sucked the sauce off the latter.

And it was at that moment he realized that the plate was empty—the dish gone. Just a bit of it was still resting in his mouth. What a mouth: a monstrous tongue and full erect nodules and ridges covering tongue and palette. A plane streaked across the sky beyond his window. He still felt strangely hungry for something simple please—at least unremarkable: something blind and bland; he scanned the kitchen. On top of the refrigerator, swaddled in a rumpled paper bag, he found a slightly stale Kaiser roll. He pulled out the firm pillow, bit in and chewed, bit in and chewed—

He sat down again, pushed away the empty plate, and closed his eyes. But in wave after wave came that image of slicing off and forking each bite into his mouth. No rest: the spongy pancake, soaked and stained with the rich sauce, edged with a thin layer of firm, chewy meat and crispy oily skin broke and reassembled before his eyes. He had eaten carefully, methodically, to retain the image of the black spiral curving into white as long as possible. He had even used his sharp paring knife to slice each piece off the torso. Now there was just an empty plate with a soggy sprig of mint, its leaves rolled up into themselves and a fine green stem, plucked free of berries. An expanding ball of warmth radiated out from his full belly. His face was flush.

Then came the first twinges of digestion. Here a slight swelling, there a teasing flurry of wings, an occasional streaming of effervescent liquid, and then somewhere deeper below, one or two sudden, though muted, pops.

He filled another glass with tap water and swallowed a full gulp. A curling tickle, a good inch below the sternum and branching to the left and right, took an ugly turn. The tickle tightened into an ever-sharper pain that soon spread across his entire abdomen. He had to groan, and with moist palm resting on tender belly, he carried himself over to the armchair. Finding the act of sitting still too strenuous, Javier sought out his bed, lay down and closed his eyes. After an hour of shifting in bed as darkness fell, food drunk Javier fell asleep.

Apart from that physical discomfort, the queasiness, followed by true nausea, somewhere in his swollen body he had been branded with a definitive marking—a graphic sign, an ever-shrinking figure, which, if he so wished it, was there to be grasped, like a hook, his hook. Once there, it would be always spinning, replacing and boring into what he had understood as his giveaway life.

Javier woke up with a yawning hunger. He stumbled into the kitchen and swung open the refrigerator door. Three eggs were waiting there in their plastic cups, the last squab, and a bottle of "Texas Hot" chili sauce. Sensing the strong pulse in his wrists, he slipped the squab out of the plastic bag, and steadied the eggs and the chili sauce on the counter.

Out came a pan.

He centered the squab in the middle of his chopping block, extending the remains of the neck and the small cartoon head at a distance from its body. With his biggest knife and strong repetitive palm thrusts he sliced the bird into thin strips from back to tail. He then cut the pieces crosswise into two. He pinched off a generous piece of butter and dropped it in the frying pan, letting it get bubbly hot before adding the squab strips in two full handfuls. A slowed sauté with a sprinkle of salt and pepper. When the delicate aroma started reaching his nose, it was time for his egg trick. He cracked all three into the same pan, breaking the shiny yellow yolks with his wooden spatula. The quickly setting liquid, like a refined mortar, filled every gap. He scrambled the eggs and bony strips of squab, at first treating it like an exotic pancake, later breaking it up to be what it was: a complex mix.

Meat cooked, eggs set, he turned it out onto a large dish and thought about inviting Yolanda: the real Yolanda from 5B. She was lovely, fat and barrel shaped: a raised barrel with a rattle of a laugh and bright warm eyes. A rotunda on two toothpick legs with beige nylon socks gathered at her ankles. She would be tickled pink to be invited to breakfast. He covered the pan to keep the stuff warm and rushed to ring her bell. Her belly still seemed to be bobbing behind her floral housedress as she arrived at the door. She loved the idea and bounced over with Javier to 5D, insisting on bringing the half dozen sausage rolls she had just brought up from the bakery. Back in the kitchen, Yolanda's warm body squeezed into the back hole of the plastic kitchen chair, tight but cozy.

Through her gaze, threaded pearly beads were drawn around whatever caught her attention.

Given the choice between Javier's dish and Yolanda's gift anyone would have discreetly selected one of those golden brown rolls. But Yolanda heaped a generous portion of the mix onto her plate squirting enough salsa all over to hide the mess below. The smell of fresh brewed coffee was filling the small kitchen, and Javier sat down to the genial scene and poured each of them a full cup.

Within a minute, Yolanda was using all her mandibles as well as the tip of her tongue to wiggle the meat free from the bone.

Th cracked bone fragment finally passed between her lips and landed back on the plate. The piece went "ping!" on the plate that Javier had just brought to the table exactly for the purpose of collecting the 17 odd skeletal fragments, and which he politely leaned in Yolanda's direction to receive the hard won first piece of extracted bone.

She chewed the slippery piece of meat—and swallowed in slow

motion with a longitudinal stretching of her gullet until the piece fell into the wide expanse of her lower body.

"*Cariño*, a tissue please—Kleenex *para los ojos.*"

Javier rummaged though all his kitchen drawers, and then rushed to the bathroom returning with a fluff of toilet tissues. Yolanda wiped the oily sweat off the flanges of her nostrils before giving her nose a good snoot. She dabbed the drops of moisture off the corners of her twinkling eyes. She had consumed the mound of egg and fowl and placed just a single sausage roll on her plate. Javier refilled her cup with the rich coffee.

She Hisses 'til He Kisses Her 'air

Every morning a young woman, wearing loose clothing she slips into upon waking, leaves her house, crosses the street, enters the playground and performs a string of physical exercises.

She understands the sequence as a kind of meditation.

She appreciates the calmness and heightened sensibility she feels these movements bring to her.

This morning she notices the same unlikely pair sitting across one another at a table set beside the playground fence. Recently, they were always there nursing beers, picking up and reading scraps of newspaper and sparring with over-exuberant gestures. As she passes by their bench, the younger one jumps out of his seat to imitate the movements of the character in his story who, at the time of the telling, is dead drunk.

She stares long enough to notice the warm reddish-tan color of his face.

The man seems too young to be sitting out the day with this overweight waster. But looking more closely into his face she can pick out signs of physical decay. His pretty blue eyes, for example, are bloodshot. Deep furrows cross his forehead. Others gather at the corner of his eyes. She finds his association with the other man unsavory. This older one is pale and flabby. She knows he follows her with a leering yet unfocused gaze. To her, the broad surface of his unshaven face is nothing more than a stubble trap for food and dirt.

She cuts across the asphalt square and then circles partially back. As usual, she takes her time, undulating her arms to emulate a river and then imitating the movements of a bird pulling in his claws. She wraps her arms around a large invisible sphere and carries it from the front to the rear tracing a continuous arc in the air. She is concentrating on what she is doing and performs as slowly as possible.

She imagines her head as an egg rolling back and forth but never fully detached from the rest of her body. Her eyes close for several perfectly concatenating moments and then open to the shells inner side. Repeatedly, her breath hits its concave surface hissing as it slips through the shell's pores. The whole thing: egg, shell, seeing, breathing, hums.

When she is finished she pauses for a moment to let the recognizable soft buzzing settle more deeply and evenly throughout her body.

"Aaah." she sighs, sensing that she has once again reached her goal of a calm, even bearing. She opens her eyes to the late morning sun appearing from behind one of the park's enclosing blank walls. The young woman moves towards the break in the playground fence.

She had wanted to avoid an encounter, scared of spilling whatever it is she is balancing in her head but it is already too late. The younger one is walking towards her cheered on by his bloated friend.

"You must be a dancer,"

"No, not really, I was just doing some morning exercise." She is beginning to tense up and wishes he would move out of the way so she could return home. But still she refuses to be rude. He has not yet actually offended her.

"I'm a good dancer, right Jim? Jim, tell her how good a dancer I am."

He grabs his friend around the middle, draws him into an embrace and demonstrates to her what he means.

"Now hold on there, Jack, I'm not that sort of guy. You let me go!" The broad face is grinning ear to ear, exposing too many stained teeth. She starts to turn away.

"Come on honey, let's give it a try, Right here. Do you need music—I don't need any. I would just really like to dance with you." he holds his arm out to her, and puts such a soft expression on his face that she can not resist. He looks straight at her, his blue eyes begging she take his hand.

It happens so slowly, maybe because of the absence of music or the unexpectedness of it all, but she moves in towards him, into his arms. They begin to dance, step by dragging step. She relishes in it, in the break in routine and in his warmth. As though the music ended they separate and she walks out of the park, crosses the street, and returns to her house feeling full and strong.

She pulls away the curtains and tries to make herself small. Standing beside the high window and the column of gathered cloth she bends down and pops the remaining soap bubbles still clinging to her freshly washed skin. Who was he? Does he live near here, for example? Who could know anything about him?

But by this time she is already too small to think up an answer.

He grew as a twig. He had friends, before, in another town and even a mother, her sister and her friends. Now his friends are throwaways. Attached, unattached, he barely needs to lift his head from the pillow to wake. He is always wide-awake, and yet still hopeless. This feeling ages him.

Attached and then unattached. His head attached to a pillow, awake. Bundled with other twigs, thrown and trucked. Delivered, unbundled indoors and set down to burn.

Part of a bundle, still himself a bundle, driven somewhere with few trees, no mothers and plenty of trash. He finds himself laid beside the trash, not really sleeping and still part of a bundle.

Picked at. Picked apart and strewn around—night: rain and rivulets channel between unbundled twigs later dry up. Twigs gathered, unburnable after dirty rain, tossed high up into the container. What is gathered is trucked. The truck driver notices twigs falling, brown-colored, while not really looking, he not wanting to catch things that fall from containers into his truck.

Part of a hill of garbage, a town dump in the city outskirts, he finally stands up and attaches himself to a truck that is driving back in. He runs away when the truck stops at a container. He avoids laying his head down and never considers returning home, even for his mother.

The egg nests in a bundle of twigs for a few moments before it cracks, its contents spilling out onto the city park pavement.

The Identity Card

... that's the title of this next story. It's about the man who keeps his pants from falling down by gathering the waist in his hand as he walks.

He's gaunt—and getting ever gaunter, lost in his pacing, which he can't for the life of him halt. He first appeared chasing a fight he wanted to have with another man to whom he must have asked the same stubborn question. He barred the man's way, by cliff-hanging onto this bulldog by a swollen spider's thread of saliva. I saw the man bare his teeth and hold an attack stance, albeit for only a hurried moment, toward his circumstantial brother, before pulling up the collar of his tight fitting coat and walking out of the station building. Later, outside on the street, he stopped me, pulling out with his free hand an ID card of a boy with a crew cut from his wallet, to ask if he was the same person as the one captured on the card. I said yes, I thought so. He had long and wavy blond hair and he wasn't smiling. With a crazed impatience, he turned his head up and back to that patch of white sky above the overpass. I continued up the street.

I thought later that he paced because of his misery. He surely wanted to be loved—even in his repulsive condition of self-doubt and uncertainty. I had answered the question he posed as if it were a detached idea. I certainly did not meet the condition I faced.

On the other hand, he could have 'let down' his pants and, if it came to that, screamed in his nudity: identity undone. Given the oversized pants, held up as they were, his composure was only partially disturbed. Something about him was still pointing in one direction or another, and then, giving up on any assurance from me, more definitively to "dear God" as the one to whom it, or he, mattered, in perpetuity.